## THE INVADERS ARE LANDING

Across the expanse of barren rock, the alien vessel rested in a pool of blue light. In that light, creatures moved like nightmare sea-things. There were six of them, knobbed and spined, moving on rows of stubbed appendages. Seven, eight, David counted; and still more poured from the vessel, working with frantic haste to erect a spidery framework.

*Brooding racks*, Dorn had said. What the term might mean, David didn't know—but in his mind was the image of seething nests of embryonic grubs, planted somewhere—far underground—to mature with terrifying speed into full-grown Invaders, superhuman, unkillable—

David caught himself. *No—not unkillable! Not quite!*

Savagely he gunned the engine, and the powerful vehicle charged from its hiding place, roaring down on the alien vessel and its nightmare crew. Through the dust-streaked windshield, David saw two of the creatures nearest the access ladder whirl and flow back up inside the hull. A moment later, the searchlight beam winked on, full in his face—dazzling, scorching hot.

David ducked down behind the dash, saw the paint bubble and smoke on the metal above him, saw the steering wheel sag and flow. The windshield blew inward, scattering gobs of molten glass. . . .

# THE INVADERS

•

## Keith Laumer

### Created by LARRY COHEN

PYRAMID BOOKS 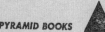 NEW YORK

THE INVADERS

A PYRAMID BOOK
First printing August, 1967

Printed in the United States of America

PYRAMID BOOKS are published by Pyramid Publications, Inc.,
444 Madison Avenue, New York, New York 10022, U.S.A.

# THE INVADERS

# PART ONE — *THE DISCOVERY*

THE XKE JAGUAR pulled to a stop at the high gate bearing the sign lettered POTOMAC MANUFAC-TURING COMPANY. A smartly uniformed plant guard stepped from the gatehouse, looked over the sleek convertible, and its broad-shouldered, sun-tanned driver.

"I'm David Vincent," the driver said. "Consulting engineer. Mr. Nagler's expecting me." He glanced at the watch on his left wrist. "I'm a few minutes early. Light traffic coming up from Washington."

"Sure, Mr. Vincent. Just a routine check. . ." The guard lifted the telephone and spoke into it. He hung up the receiver and nodded, touched the switch which cycled the barred gate open.

"Straight ahead to the main building. Mr. Nagler's office is just off the entrance lobby."

"Thanks." Vincent wheeled the powerful little car past the large brick gatehouse, pulled into a visitor's slot near the flagpole. Inside, a shapely receptionist with platinum tinted hair rose to lead him across to the door marked M. G. NAGLER—GENERAL MAN-AGER—PRIVATE.

"If you're here to sell him anything, you picked a

7

bad day, Mr. Vincent," she murmured. "Late party at the country club last night." She adjusted her hornrim spectacles, which seemed to be of plain glass. If they were intended to add seriousness to her mischievous face, David thought, they were a failure.

"Thanks for the warning," he said. "I'll try not to make any loud noises." He gave her a half wink and went in.

Nagler was a tall, lanky man, with thinning hair and large, features, now wearing an expression of patient suffering.

"Mr. Vincent," he greeted his visitor, waving him to a chair. "Nice to see you. I hope you'll be able to help us here at Potomac. It's a case of changing markets, competition. An old story to you, I suppose. But we've got to diversify or go under. That means expansion. And capital's a big problem."

"I've studied the data you supplied the home office," Vincent said. "I think I have a few ideas. Suppose we take a look at the plant before I go into them any further."

"Fine." Nagler spoke to his secretary on the intercom, then led Vincent out along a flower-bordered walk across a neatly tended lawn, into a cavernous, noisy building, murkily lit by sunlight angling in through high windows. There were long rows of turret lathes manned by serious machinists, banks of massive milling machines, a row of power saws, each adding its note to the overall noise. Farther on, giant plastics moulding machines radiated heat and harsh chemical odors. With Nagler at his side, Vincent moved slowly along the aisles, carefully studying the details of the factory's operation.

". . . we're bursting our seams as it is," Nagler was saying; but Vincent had stopped, was watching a left-fingered woman at an assembly table. She was tucking copper wires inside a small metal and plastic assembly, an endless supply of which were moving past her on a conveyor belt.

"May I?" David said, and plucked one of the finished assemblies from the line. It was about the size of a goose egg—an egg with one end lopped off, flattened sides, holes of various sizes bored in its smooth curves. The material was smooth, dark blue plastic with a slick, tingly feel. At one end was a metal rim with recessed mounting lugs. Inside the open end was a maze of printed circuitry, the glint of transistors, the bright colors of tiny condensers.

"A special-order item," Nagler said. "A nuisance— even at the price. They require a whole new manufacturing setup, their own assembly line, special training. All for what may turn out to be a one-time order. But we can't afford to turn away the business . . ."

"What's it for?" David asked. His tone was intent, serious.

Nagler shrugged. "A sub-assembly. A firm called Electronic Components placed the order, then thousand units, very complex specifications, too; immediate delivery. We quoted them—"

"Just this one item? Not the entire apparatus?" David cut into the stream of talk.

"That's right. It's a common occurrence in our line of business, of course. But the expense—"

"Where is this Electronic Components company located?"

"Eh? Why, I'd have to check that. West Coast, I believe." Nagler looked at Vincent. "Why do you ask? As I said, this is just a one-time special order."

"You never can tell what might be important, Mr. Nagler." David smiled disarmingly. "When we get back to the office, I'd like to have that address, if you don't mind."

But, half an hour later in Nagler's office, the file clerk shook her head.

"It's very strange, sir," she said. "All we have is the post office address—Box 1009, Wheaton. No mention in the correspondence of where the plant is located."

"I wonder if I might keep this?" David held up the device he had plucked from the assembly line.

"Certainly, if it's of any use to you." Nagler frowned. "But frankly, I don't see what bearing it has on our main problem here . . ."

"As to that, I think I have good news for you, Mr. Nagler," Vincent said, pocketing the apparatus. "I think we can solve your problem with no more than the addition of a new production control center and a new wing on building five. . . ."

2

Two hours later, Vincent parked his car in the hotel lot, paused at the cigaret counter for a pack of the cigarillos. He often smoked them when on long road trips which kept him from the comfort of his bachelor apartment in the new Columbia Towers in Alexandria. The sales girl, a slim red-head, returned his change with a lingering glance. It expressed unqualified approval of his lean, well-chiselled face, his short-cut blond hair, the rugged physique apparent under his well-tailored suit. He gave her a smile that was no more than friendly as he turned to the elevators. There was no time now to strike up new acquaintances, he reflected with wry regret as the swift car bore him upwards. Or was there? Was the whole idea that had been growing in his mind these past weeks no more than an over-active imagination?

Maybe he ought to invite the red-head to dinner, relax, forget the whole thing. . . .

But the bulge in his pocket was real. And until he had satisfied his engineers curiosity, he would have to hold back the urge to sociability.

In his room, Vincent switched on the lamp over the desk, placed the egg-shaped object in the center of the blotter. From his suitcase, he took three other objects, placed them beside the one he had acquired at the Potomac Company. They were completely un-like—yet strangely similar in an indefinable way. As if, David told himself, they were parts of the same finished apparatus. . . .

One was a pale yellow rod of the same semigloss finish plastic as the blue egg-shape, about five inches long, as thick as a fountain pen. Another was cherry red, rectangular, two inches long by an inch wide, wafer thin, with metal contacts visible at one end. The third was an irregularly formed casting, pale green, fitted with a button which slid, with faint clicks, along a graduated scale. Each bore either holes or small protrusions, presumably designed to allow attachment to some other part. The trick was, David reflected, to discover exactly how they fitted togeth-er—if indeed his hunch was correct. So far, he had had no luck; but with the new part—perhaps he'd find the answer. There was a hole in the latter which appeared to be about the size of the yellow rod. He tried it—and felt a surge of excitement as it slid smoothly in, locked in place with a soft click. Tugging failed to remove it; it was in to stay.

"Lesson number one," David murmured to himself. "Once in, it stays in. . ." He studied the other parts, comparing their contours. The hollow in one end of the green casting looked about right to receive the blue egg-shape; and the studs on the red wafer matched the perforations on the opposite side of the egg. He was right, his new acquisition was the key part to which all the others fitted.

He leaned back in the chair, lit a cigaret and considered the array of cryptic items before him. The first to catch his eye had been the yellow rod. It had been the material, more than any curiosity as to its function, which had attracted his notice: tough, conductive, machinable under specific conditions, taking a temper like metal. The material had been supplied, along with the plans and specifications for the rods. Marvelous stuff, the plant manager had said sadly; but unobtainable in bulk, according to the supplier. Probably one of those German imports, he had guessed.

David had taken along one of the rods, run tests on the plastic—and discovered just how fantastic the material was. Once tempered, no temperature he had been able to obtain with a late model electronic crucible had touched it. No blade would mark it, no solvent etch it.

And then, a week later, hundreds of miles distant, he had seen the same, unmistakable plastic being formed into the red wafers. Then the green objects had shown up, at a small factory near Chicago. In each case, the only address given had been a small-town post office box. And now, after a month of discreet search, the blue ovoid had turned up. His boss, peppery old General Moore, USA Ret, founder and head of Modern Industrial Designs—20th Century—MID-20th to its familiars—would have hit the ceiling, David reflected, if he had any inkling as to why his star plant consultant had suddenly developed a fondness for personally carrying out preliminary surveys of minor remodelling jobs spread across half the country.

And it was still a good question; why should he have taken such a consuming interest in the fact that small factories, unknown to each other, were turning out uniform orders of ten thousand each of small, different, but related items? It was a question David could not have answered, he admitted to himself. But it was part and parcel of the fact that his own peculiar talent—the talent that had led him to the top of his field in the few short years since his graduation *cum laude* from MIT—was the ability to spot relationships among things that looked different whether they were factory flow lines, or, as now, various parts of a single assembly.

David took paper and pen from the desk drawer, arranged the objects in the various positions with quick, practiced strokes, he sketched the results. He tried and rejected half a dozen possibilities before he arrived at what seemed the most likely solution: The wafer atop the egg shape, opposite the green item he had come to think of as the grip, with the yellow rod projecting in front. The pegs and holes matched, each part would nestle snugly against the other—not that he had tried them. The result, he saw, with a grin, looked remarkably like a Buck Rogers Space Gun. But it was obvious that something was missing. There was a circle of small holes around the base of the yellow rod, and the leads from the wafer dangled, making contact with nothing. Using a micrometer, David checked clearances and spacings, began carefully sketching the probable form of the missing part.

Slowly, it took shape: a cluster of rods, with a ring at one end, heavy leads passing back on each side to

fit the holes beneath the egg shape, other leads which
snapped into the wafer above. The result was more
ray-gunlike than ever. He shook his head and smiled
at his over-active imagination. The thing was probably a new heatless soldering iron, or light-duty
welder; or a signalling apparatus, or even some sort of
hand-drill. Since he couldn't see inside the plastic
casings, he still had no idea of the thing's function. . . .

But something could be done about that. Mid-
20th's labs were the most modern and complete in the
United States—probably in the world. There were
tests he could run, and analyses, using the electron
scope and X-ray and even gamma-ray scanning techniques. There were two more plants to visit on this
swing through the district. By day after tomorrow
he'd be back at home base. He could run his tests
then, settle his curiosity once and for all, and forget
the matter.

With that decided, he felt a sense of relief, as if a
deep problem had been solved—or at least deferred.
He placed the parts in his suitcase, showered and
dressed and went down to dinner.

## CHAPTER TWO

Two DAYS LATER, as he was completing the final in-
spection of the trip at the Ultimate Tool and Die
Works, a medium-sized manufacturing plant near
Fort Wayne, David Vincent paused, took a folded
paper from his pocket.

"Just as a matter of curiosity, Mr. Winthrop," he said to the company president escorting him, "have you ever seen an item resembling this?" He showed the man the sketch he had made of the missing component. The latter blinked at it, turned it upside down.

"Why, as a matter of—" Winthrop broke off as the tall man who had been following silently a few feet behind stepped forward and unceremoniously plucked the paper from his hand.

"As to your security chief, sir, I advise against answering Mr. Vincent's questions," the man said in a harsh-clipped voice. He had a narrow, curiously unlined face, pale, almost ochre eyes, a thin mouth. His black hair, combed back in a patent-leather wing, looked like a badly made wig. His eyes flicked to the paper; he folded it deliberately, tucked it into a pocket. "We handle a number of Defense Department contracts here," he said curtly to Vincent.

The company officer's face flushed. "Mr. Vincent is here—at a cost of one hundred dollars per day, I might remind you Dorn—to study our operation! I intend to answer his questions to the best of my ability—"

"Not when the national security is involved," Dorn said flatly.

"National security? What's the national security got to do with an order from Technical Associates, Incorporated?"

"A company which specifically ordered you to divulge no information to anyone!" Dorn rapped.

"Ordered! I'll do the ordering here!" Winthrop snapped. "And I'll observe their *request* insofar as it doesn't interfere with our own operations!"

"Are you certain the firm you mentioned has no

connection with secret government work?" Dorn's face was taut with what looked like barely suppressed fury.

"Well—no, I'm not—but—inasmuch as I have no official directive—"

"It is not necessary to tell Mr. Vincent any more than he already knows in the matter," Dorn rasped.

"I'll be the judge of that," the executive snapped.

"I advise you to consider carefully before you say more," Dorn said, in a curiously flat tone. His eyes held those of his employer. His skin, Vincent noted, seemed dry and lifeless. Something about the man was repellent. Under that fierce gaze, the older man's eyes quailed.

"Well—since you feel so strongly about it . . ." Avoiding David's look, Winthrop brushed past and through the door. Dorn turned to David with an impatient gesture.

"We will go now, Mr. Vincent."

"I'll have my sketch back first," David said.

"That's not possible," Dorn rapped.

"It's my property, Dorn," David said quietly. "I want it."

"It's nothing—merely that we resent prying." Dorn took the paper from his pocket—and ripped it across, again, turned and tossed the scraps into a waste disposal conveyor where they were instantly whirled away. David reached out, caught the security chief's arm. Instantly, violently, the man tore free. David fought to keep his expression calm, after the shock of that momentary contact. Under his hand, the other's arm had been as hard as oak—and hot! Scaldingly, impossibly hot! And even now, standing three feet from that mask-like face, he could feel the heat radiating from his features, as from an open furnace door.

"Never touch me!" Dorn hissed.

"Thanks," David said. "That tells me what I wanted

to know." He turned and went through the door, feeling Dorn's eyes following him like aimed guns.

2

David stayed at the factory for another two hours, finishing the compilation of data needed for his engineering study of the plant's operation. The company president made no mention of his security chief's strange behavior, nor did David refer to the matter.

It was late afternoon when he left the plant, with a two-hour drive via freeway ahead. Usually, he enjoyed an opportunity to let the swift Jag out, but this time the prospect of the high-pressure trip, weaving in and out of speeding traffic, was distasteful. He had too much to think about. Or was it all his imagination? Perhaps Dorn was just overeager, wanting to impress his boss with his zeal.

Ahead, a highway marker indicated State Road 27, branching off from the freeway approach. On sudden impulse, David cut the wheel, a moment later was skimming along a winding, two lane road, smooth-surfaced, empty of traffic. This was better; now he could think without pressure.

What was there, really, to give him this queasy, restless feeling under the ribs? A series of strange sub-assemblies, ordered by mysterious firms, all previously unknown to him in spite of his wide experience in the small manufacturing field, all with oddly anonymous mailing addresses; the curiously gun-like form of the finished product; and the swift, hostile reaction of the man Dorn. As for the latter's apparent abnormal body heat—it had probably been an illusion; a combination of the sense of warmth generated by hot tempers, and an accidental blast of air from some open furnace door behind him. Not that there had been any such furnace in sight. . . .

The sun was behind the trees now, shedding long, slanting rays across ordered fields, coloring the distant farmhouses a ruddy pink. Overhead, a helicopter whiffled on its way a few hundred feet above the ground. David drew a deep breath, pressed on the accelerator. It was a beautiful world, a good life. He was young—barely 28—with the best job in the world, health, no responsibilities except for himself. . . .

Somehow, the nagging sense of doubt, suspicion—it was hard to pin a name on it—sprang from that same sense of responsibility. It was as though some indefinable threat hung over . . . not merely himself, but this whole peaceful scene.

He shook his head impatiently. He was imagining things, building what was probably a perfectly innocent matter up into a dark conspiracy. He should put the whole matter out of his mind, call Marcia when he reached home, have a night on the town. Tomorrow, in the bright light of morning, it would all seem like what it no doubt was: a wild fancy brought on by overwork and too much of his own company.

But even as he relaxed, a vagrant thought struck him. He remembered Winthrop glancing at the sketch before Dorn had seized it. And he had said—what?"

*Why—as a matter of fact. . .*

David nodded to himself. The man had been about to say that he recognized the sketch. And if that were so—there might be more information in the company's files—perhaps complete plans and specifications. If so, that would end the mystery. And he might as well see the thing through now as lie awake tonight thinking about it. David braked, swung the small car

in a U turn, and headed back toward the Utlimate
Tool and Die Company.

3

There were cars clustered near the junction where
State Road 27 joined U.S. 41. Two Maryland State
Highway Patrolmen waved Vincent down. Ahead,
smoke wafted upward from a burned-out wreck, lying
smashed against the abutment. A blanket-covered
body lay on the grassy bank beside it.

"What happened?" David called.

The police eyed him non-commitally, one coming up
on either side of the car.

"Notice you have a DC plate," one said. "What
brings you here?"

"Business," Vincent said. Across the road, the odor
of burning tires was rank. There were a dozen cars
halted, their drivers craning for a view.

"Kind of an out-of-the-way route for a businessman
in a hurry." the other cop suggested.

"What makes you think I'm in a hurry?" David
asked, smiling slightly.

"Don't get tough," the first cop started—

"Lay off him, Chuck," the other trooper said. "This
can looks like it's in a hurry when it's sitting still." He
gave Vincent a severe look. "You see anything out of
the ordinary around here in the last few minutes?"

David shook his head. "Why" He glanced at the
wrecked car. It was a heavy black limousine, the
paint still gleaming where it had not been burnt and
blistered.

"Bypassers reported an explosion just before it hit,"
the first cop said. "We—

"That's enough," his partner growled. "Probably just

a blow-out. You say nothing, eh?" he frowned at Vincent.

David shook his head again—then hesitated.

"There was a helicopter," he said. "I thought it was probably a crop duster."

The two policemen exchanged glances. One turned and walked to the squad car, began operating the radio, while the other quizzed Vincent as to the details of the machine he had seen.

"OK, you can go along," he said when he finished. "Maybe we'll call you."

David nodded. "Any idea who the driver was?"

"Sure," the cop said, wagging his head. "Fine man plenty of money, too. Winthrop was his name. Manager of the plant just up the road."

## CHAPTER THREE

ACCIDENT—OR INTENTION? David Vincent asked himself the question as he drove slowly toward the distant, looming shape of the factory he had left less than an hour earlier. It was hard to picture Winthrop, the well-fed, competent executive as the still figure under the blanket. As for himself ... he had changed his route, twice, unexpectedly. Was that the reason that he wasn't dead himself now? He shook his head impatiently. He was developing a morbid imagination. There was nothing—nothing whatever that would stand up under close scrutiny as anything other than hunch, coincidence, suspicion. And of what? He didn't know. And now Winthrop would never tell him. As for Dorn—maybe he should have mentioned him to the police. But what would he have said? That the man had torn up his sketch? It sounded flimsy, unconvincing, laughable. But regardless of how it sounded, the feeling was there, gnawing at him, growing, that all was not well....

David drove past the plant gates. They were closed, locked, the big security lights already on in the early twilight. He wondered if the personnel knew of the death of the manager—if Dorn knew. Somehow, chillingly, he was convinced that he did. But again—what good was groundless suspicion..?

But if he had grounds; if there was something more concrete to work on, some evidence of—whatever was going on. And if there was such evidence—it would be there; in the files of the Ultimate Tool and Die Works. Dorn would never give him a glimpse inside the walls. But what if he didn't bother with knocking at the gate?

There was a side road a quarter of a mile ahead, shadowy under dark trees. David pulled the car in, switched off, sat in the dark, studying the lights of the plant, listening—for what, he could not have said. He wanted a cigaret, but even that small glow would have been too conspicuous now. Suddenly he felt very much alone, vulnerable, like a secret agent deep behind the enemy lines.

*I should get out of here*, he told himself. *Report what I've seen to General Moore. Let him take it from there. He still knew people in high places...*

But there was still nothing to tell—nothing concrete. And there was just one way to change that. He'd have to go in—over, under, or around Dorn's security system—and see for himself.

David Vincent stepped from the car, pushed

through the dense hedge and started toward the dark walls of the factory.

2

It took David forty minutes to scout the ten-acre walled enclosure. At the southwest corner of the outer compound, a clump of poplar trees grew close to the ten-foot barrier. He scaled one, carefully lowered himself to the top of the wall. From here he could see the plant guard lounging at the main gate, a watchman with a leashed dog making the rounds on the far side of the enclosure. Neither was near enough to be an immediate danger. David dropped to the grassy strip below. Two minutes later, he was in a narrow passage between a warehouse and an open materials shed. Harsh mercury vapor lamps shed a cold blue radiance on the pavement ahead. A narrow band of shadow ran under an overhang protecting loading platforms. In its shelter he crossed to the side door of an outlying wing of the main building. The lock was a stout Yale model. Vincent smiled grimly. Locks had always been a hobby of his, along with anything else mechanical. He bent the piece of baling wire he had picked up behind the warehouse into a hook of peculiar shape, inserted it, tickled the tumblers. There was a soft click and the door swung in. Another minute's work and he had shorted the inductance-type sensor guarding the entry, the details of which he had automatically noted while studying the plans of the building earlier in the day.

In the faint light reflecting through the windows, he crossed a wide office along an aisle between typist's desks and filing cabinets. The papers he wanted would not be here, but in Winthrop's office. He went through the double swinging doors into a tiled hall.

The building was utterly silent. The gold lettering on the manager's office door gleamed dully at him— almost, the thought came to him, like a silent appeal.

Using the wire, he opened the locked door, locked it after him. The inner door stood half open. On Winthrop's desk, a briefcase lay in the center of the blotter, open, empty. Somehow it gave the impression that its owner had left in haste. . . .

The filing cabinet in the corner was an expensive executive model, with individual drawer locks plus a locking bar secured by a heavy combination padlock. This, David saw, would require more than a twist of wire to handle. He spun the dial once or twice to get the feel of it, then settled down, his ear to the metal door, delicately turning the knob with sensitive fingers.

Twenty agonizingly slow minutes later, the final digit snicked in place and the lock dropped open. Another five minutes with a straightened paperclip, and the drawers slid out. Slowly, methodically, David went through the packed folders, searching for any reference to Technical Associates, Incorporated—the firm Winthrop had referred to before Dorn had intervened. Once feet sounded in the hall outside, the click of a dog's claws; the outer door rattled as the watchman tried it. David held his breath until the slow tread moved on. His scent, familiar from his visit, had not betrayed him. Then the search continued.

It was almost a full hour before a familiar outline caught his eye, one of a sheaf of thumb-marked prints in a file marked: BID DOCUMENTS—PENDING. It was unmistakably the missing component. The design was remarkably like the reconstruction David had sketched. The leads to the 'grip' were housed in channels along the side of the unit, he saw, and there was an additional small protuberance at the top, and a number of metal fittings which might have been sights. But as for function—that was as big a mystery as ever.

He put the folder on the desktop in a narrow band of brighter light from the outside, leafed through page after page of complex wiring diagrams, special alloying and forming instructions, technical notation. He frowned as he noted the columns of cryptic indications: core gradient, 4.0967; boundary layer permeability, .0098; flux density, alpha range, 14,000—26,-500. . . .

If these were engineering specifications, they were of a kind unknown to modern industry. The circuitry made no sense. The machine tolerances called for were of an incredible precision. No wonder the Ultimate Tool and Die Works was still holding the documents in their PENDING file. The job called for techniques and equipment more appropriate to a major research laboratory than to a commercial firm.

There was a copying machine in the corner of the room. David switched it on, in ten minutes had duplicated the mysterious papers. He returned the originals to the file, closed and locked the drawer, wiped away all fingerprints. With his copies safely tucked away in an inner pocket, he turned to the door—and froze as the outer office door clicked and swung in. David flattened himself against the wall, shielded by a filing cabinet beside the inner door. The light snapped on in the outer office. David held his breath as a man appeared in the doorway, outlined against the glare behind him. It was Dorn.

The security chief came into the room, brushed past not a yard from where David stood in the dense shadow of the cabinet. A second man followed him; a tall, lean man in a plant policeman's uniform. Dorn half turned; the angular planes of his face caught the light from beyond the door. His mouth opened—and abruptly, shockingly, a harsh, metallic buzzing issued from it. David stood rigid, listening, as the guard buzzed a reply. Dorn went to the filing cabinet, opened it, took out a folder which David instantly recognized as the one he had just duplicated. Again the grotesque, incredible exchange of buzzes—like the hum of insects, grossly magnified. Then Dorn closed the drawer, replaced the lock. The two men left the room. The light switched off, the outer door banged shut behind them. David let out a long breath. It had been close—terribly close. And now he had to get clear with his trophy, or it was all wasted. And somehow, without putting it in words, he knew now that what was at stake was more than the career of a consulting engineer named David Vincent—or even his life. In the alien buzzings, the glint of light from the flat, remorseless eyes of the pair he had watched at close range, there was a nameless menace that closed about his heart like an icy hand, seeming to threaten the very world he lived in.

3

He left the building by the same door through which he had entered. A hundred yards distant, the watchman tried a shed door, his dog snuffling at his feet. David ducked out, reached the temporary safety of the alley running beside the warehouse. A moment later, he was at the wall, a sheer, ten-foot barrier, with no friendly tree now to help him. Here in the deep gloom, it was difficult to see the top. He jumped, his fingers brushed the coping, and he dropped back—and metal clattered as his foot struck piled angle iron. At once, the dog bayed, sounding

dangerously close. David groped in the darkness at
his feet; his fingers found a length of heavy I-beam,
scaled with rust. He lifted one end; it was incredibly
heavy. Muscles straining, he raised the six foot rail,
leaned it against the wall. It was a poor ladder, but
better than none. He gripped it; scrambled up, got a
foothold, reached the top of the wall. As he pulled
himself up, feet sounded in the alley mouth, the
eager whine of the dog. A man burst into view,
holding back the straining animal, a huge black and
tan bloodhound. The beam of a powerful flashlight
speared out, played across the weed-grown ground,
the jumbled scrap iron—and found the end of the
upraised I-beam. The man took a step forward, his
hand darting for the holstered pistol at his hip. With
a final lunge, David gained the top of the wall—and
the massive steel section, unbalanced by the thrust,
slid, grating along the rough brickwork. The man
scrambled back, yanking the gun free; his foot
caught, and he went down on his back—and the
scream in his throat choked off as the ponderous steel
beam thundered down across his chest. The dog
snarled and leaped, fell back with a yelp as the leash
brought him up short. Crouched atop the wall, David
stared down horrified at the sight of the victim pinned
under the rusted metal. And then the fallen guard
moved, his hands groping over the surface of the metal.
He gripped, pushed—and the thousand pound beam
lifted, fell aside as if it were a cardboard mock-up. The
man rose, staggered for a moment, then stooped, re-
covered his light. All this in a frozen, timeless moment.

Then, as the light flicked upward, David turned,
jumped down into darkness, and ran for the distant
line of trees. And behind him, the dog bayed, like a
wolf howling at the moon.

# CHAPTER FOUR

EIGHTEEN HOURS had passed since the night raid on the Ultimate Tool and Die Works. In a shabby hotel room in South Chicago, David Vincent, for the hundredth time, pushed aside the tantalizing sheets of paper bearing the designs for the mysterious apparatus, baffled. All his training in engineering, his intuitive ability to fathom the workings of complex machines and systems, were helpless before the overwhelming strangeness, illogicality, the seemingly meaningless complexity of the device—just as the smooth plastic cases of the other assemblies in his suitcase were proof against his every effort to open them. He was at an impasse; this road led him nowhere. He must, he knew now, have help. And there was one man to whom his thoughts went: Dr. Albert Lieberman, research physicist on the staff of the University of Chicago, and his good friend and former classmate.

David almost smiled as the knowledge came clearly in focus at last; he must, subconsciously, have known all along that in the end he would turn to Al. All the while he had been driving hell-for-leather away from the factory, keeping to back roads, pausing to listen for sounds of pursuit, he had known. That was why he was here, less than fifteen miles from the Lieberman house, instead of at the other end of the country.

He packed away the drawing, sluiced down his face with cold water. His features stared back at him from the mirror, hollow-cheeked, drawn, after nearly forty hours without sleep. And when had he eaten last? A paper plate, a crumpled paper napkin on the bedside table reminded him of a greasy hamburger consumed twelve hours ago, when he had checked in, just after dawn. By now, back at MID-20th, General Moore would be pacing the floor, pounding desks, demanding to know what had happened to his overdue employee—and the half million dollars in design proposals he should have brought in, a day ago. David shook his head, ran his fingers through his rumpled hair. Perhaps the thing to do would have been to call Moore, tell him the story—but somehow, instinct had led him here—in secret. And now he was committed. To report in now, with nothing except a sheaf of stolen drawings and an incoherent tale—

No, he would have to see Al. Between them, with Lieberman's vast theoretical knowledge linked to David's quick engineer's grasp of the practical, they would deduce the nature and function of the machine that was being so ingeniously assembled—in the tens of thousands—by unsuspecting manufacturers all across the Eastern seaboard.

The room clerk bid him farewell with a grunt as he paid his bill; he tilted his bald head toward a side door in reply to David's question. Beyond the greasy glass door, it was early evening; a grey, misty sky hung low over the grimed street. David's car, parked at the curb, even coated as it was with greyish mud from the long run on unpaved roads, was incongruously elegant in the drab setting. David checked as he was about to step from the door. A man stood against a building front near the car; a tall, lean, angular-faced man, in a dark suit. For a heart-stopping instant, he thought it was Dorn. Then the man glanced his way. It wasn't the security officer—but it might have been his brother. The cold, flat eyes flicked past. David stepped back past the desk, around it into a narrow passage leading to the back. The clerk swivelled to follow him, spat out a toothpick.

"Hey!" he snarled. "Where you think you're going?"

"Cops," Vincent said tersely. "You want 'em in here?"

The man narrowed his eyes. "Through the kitchen," he grunted. "There's a fence a guy could get over." He spat on the floor. "Cops!" He turned away, dismissing the incident. Half a minute later, David stepped out between overflowing garbage cans into a narrow, crooked alley, a dark canyon between blackened walls. Weak, yellow light leaked from behind a broken shade in a window above, showed him a sagging board fence. He went over it, adding new stains and tears to those that had already reduced his once-sharp outfit to the semblance of a hobo's rags. At that, it was as good a disguise as any—if he really needed concealment—if the whole thing wasn't his imagination. But that was a question he could settle soon now. Al would be able to help him.

*If anyone could*, the thought came as a chill weight in his mind as he made his way across the strewn bottle and cans of a vacant lot.

2

It took David Vincent over two hours, via foot, bus, and for the last stretch, taxi, to reach the cavernous, elm-shaded house on the quiet side street near the campus. He studied it from the sidewalk, noted the light in an upstairs window. It was early, but Al was a man with no fixed hours. It was hard to say whether he was going to bed or just rising.

David went up the steps, rang. He waited, feeling

exposed, vulnerable. A light went on beyond the stained glass fanlight. The door opened, and Al's familiar seamed, lantern-jawed face appeared.

"David! What in the name of—what's happened to you, boy?" Lieberman pulled him inside, asking ten questions at once. Briefly, tersely, David explained. His friend listened silently, attentively, his eyes on David's face.

"You say you ... stole these drawings, Dave?" he asked as Vincent finished his account.

"That's right—and came close to killing a man in the process. Maybe I'm out of my mind. Maybe the thing is nothing but a new model egg-beater. But I don't think so, Al. I'm scared. Scared all the way through."

"You—David Vincent—the toughest line-backer that ever wore a Phi Beta Kappa key? Scared? The lad that won more decorations in Viet Nam than—"

"This isn't Viet Nam, Al. It's worse. Much worse. Or maybe it's nothing. I admit I'm operating on instinct. But you're the one who can tell me." He took the drawings from his pocket. "Look at these and then tell me I need a long rest."

Silently, Lieberman looked over the papers. His frown deepened as he leafed through them. He paused, staring at a page filled with chemical process-flow notations. At the next—a sheet filled with cryptic columns which David had found totally incomprehensible—his face stiffened.

"My God!" he blurted.

"Well, how about it," David asked tensely. "Can you make anything of it?"

"I hope I'm wrong, David," Lieberman said in a strangely choked voice. "I hope I'm wrong. But if this is what it looks like—the worse things you've imagined are just happy day-dreams compared with the truth!"

3

The basement of Al Lieberman's sprawling forty-year old house was given over to a complex of private laboratories fitted out with the most advanced equipment available to modern physics and chemistry—sciences which, as Lieberman said, were facets of a single body of phenomena. His shops, in fact, included apparatus, particularly analytical devices, superior to anything commercially available—devices designed and built by himself, following principles of his own invention. In the entire country—perhaps in all the world—there was no single physicist possessed of more virtuosity in his chosen field than this man.

Together, he and David Vincent examined the four metal-and-plastic objects laid out under a stark fluorescent light on a stone-topped table. Lieberman pared over the drawings of the fifth part, nodding in agreement as David pointed out what he had deduced of the order of assembly.

"It appears to me that we have the entire aggregation here," he said thoughtfully. "I suggest that before going any further, we see what we can find out about the portions already in hand."

For the remainder of the day, the two men subjected the enigmatic objects to test after test, first confirming David's previous impression that the material was impervious to any force they could bring to bear on it, then proceeding to probe into the inner circuitry by means of a variety of electrical and magnetic impulses.

"The picture I'm getting makes no sense at all,

David," the physicist shook his head wearily as they consumed their tenth—or twentieth cup of coffee.

"This material would appear, from the notes, to be a metallo-organic alloy, formed under intense pressures into a sort of pre-crystalline state, then, after tempering, assuming a collapsed-lattice structure of incredible stability. And as for the circuitry inside the things—I just don't know enough! Inductance, reluctance, capacitance, resistances in the thousands of ohms at one current level, dropping to zero half an ampere away." He picked up the blue, egg-shaped segment, the yellow rod still firmly welded in place. "I detect what appears to be a tremendously powerful, poleless, linear magnetic field here—if such a thing is possible—oriented along the axial line. But as to power source—nothing. And the contacts at the end seem functionless. I'm afraid we've struck a dead end. There's nothing here that fits into any theoretical conception of matter-energy relationships I've ever encountered—or imagined. The only faint hint of familiarity is in some of the more abstruse mathematical fancies of Brumbacher and Polzansky regarding n-dimensional space."

"You said before that you had an idea; that it suggested something to you."

Lieberman flipped back the top pages of the sheaf of specifications. "This, you mean. But I must be mistaken. These are standard, if little known, notations used in the field of sub-nuclear physics. As combined here they seem to imply . . . well, possibilities that are a Pandora's box! If powers like these are ever unleashed—I shudder to think of the consequences!"

"Someone, apparently, plans to unleash them," David said flatly.

"David, we've got to go to the AEC, to the President if necessary! The implications of this—"

"How many men are there in the AEC who'd understand the implications?" David cut in.

"Why—I suppose any competent physicist—once he had examined certain formulations of mine—"

"Without your formulations—how many?"

"As to that . . ." Lieberman ran his thick, skilled fingers through his rough, greying hair. "Frankly, Dave—I don't know. At the risk of sounding like an impossible egoist—not many, I'm afraid. Perhaps none."

"So—that leaves it up to us. And Al," David added softly, "I don't think we have much time."

"What?" Lieberman blinked at Vincent over the glasses he donned for close work. "You mean—you think they—whoever they are—might have followed you here? Might interfere?"

"If they could. Even if I've succeeded in throwing them off temporarily, they might still manage to trace me. And in any event—somewhere, they're going ahead with the manufacture of this infernal machine—whatever it is. I think we've pretty well established that it's not an orange squeezer."

Lieberman nodded, looking grave. "You're right, of course," he said briskly.

"That leaves us just one course, Al," David said gravely.

"You mean. . . ?" Lieberman left the question hanging in the air.

David nodded. "We'll have to set to work and manufacture the missing part ourselves."

4

For seven days and seven nights, hardly pausing for food, kept in a state of artificial alertness by special nerve-drugs supplied by the physicist, pausing only for brief catnaps, necessary to prevent breakdown, David Vincent and Albert Lieberman labored, first to synthesize the plastic material in accordance with the stolen specifications, then to form the subminiature circuitry—which in itself involved the painstaking fabrication, by hand, of a variety of components of unknown function—and at last, with the maze of wires in place, to seal the housing and attach the external fittings.

"That's it," Lieberman said at last. "I don't know what it is, but it's what the plans and specifications call for." His voice was hoarse with weariness.

"Then the next step is to fit it together."

Lieberman hesitated. "First, I'd like to run some checks on the new circuits. Perhaps, in conjunction with the findings from the others, the computer can tell us something." He referred to the compact, ultrasophisticated differential integrator which occupied one wall of the lab—the product of his own cybernetic researches. But hours later, the last line of investigation exhausted, he shook his head in defeat.

"It's entirely outside the competence of conventional physics, David," he stated flatly. "I'd conclude the entire matter was an elaborate hoax, if it weren't for one or two dazzling insights I've glimpsed here, into whole new realms of matter-energy manipulation. According to this last read-out, once assembled and activated, the thing should emit a tightly focussed beam of what I can only describe as negative space—a meaningless concept—"

"Just a minute," Vincent cut in. "Negative space? What's that?"

"A purely theoretical concept. You've heard of antimatter, of course—again, only a hypothetical conception, but possible, within the framework of Einsteinian physics. If normal matter and anti-matter should come in contact, mutual annihilation would result, with a vast release of energy. Negative space, in theory, would be the matrix in which anti-matter might come into existence. . ." The physicist's voice faded off; a speculative look came into his eyes. "Of course, if negative space should be created—even in a volume as finite as a thin core within the magnetic pencil— then air molecules entering the closed continuum would undergo a transformation to anti-matter. With the magnetic beam again buffering them, they would be aligned along the axis, and expelled with tremendous velocity, driven by the energy release. . ." Lieberman whirled to the table, seized pencil and paper, began jotting furiously. Fifteen minutes later, his face rigid with excitement—and other emotions: fear, incredulity, wonder—he looked up at David, standing tensely by.

"Dave," he whispered, "if this thing works—and it might—this is the most unbelievable weapon ever put in the hands of irresponsible humanity!"

"What is it, Al," David asked urgently. "Tell me what it is!

"A Buck Rogers gun, you called it." Lieberman barked a laugh, without humor. "You weren't far off. This thing will create a field which destroys the interatomic bonds of any matter it impinges upon, converting the target into pure energy—then absorb the energy in a matter-anti-matter transformation."

"In other words?" David prompted.

"In other words," Lieberman echoed huskily, "a disintegrator."

# CHAPTER FIVE

"We can't assemble and test this thing," Al Lieberman said. "It's too dangerous. God knows what the result might be: an explosion of titanic proportions, a self-propagating energy vortex—you name it. We have to go to higher authority, call in all the brainpower at the country's command to check and recheck, set up the proper safeguards."

"All right; now that we have something to show, I'm in agreement," David said. "I suppose the FBI is the logical place to start."

"Right. We'll call the local office, and put the matter in their hands."

David made the call. A calm, well-modulated, masculine voice listened to his brief statement—David made no mention of the precise nature of the 'vital information' in his possession—and agreed to send a four-man escort to the address immediately.

"Please remain indoors, and make no other calls until the agents arrive," the FBI man said. "Don't answer the doorbell, unless you hear three short rings followed by a long one."

"That's that," David said. "In a few minutes it will all be over." He looked at the scattered parts lying on the table; in themselves so innocent, but together, potentially possessed of a power which, in the wrong hands, could destroy any army sent against it—and with it, the entire structure of world society.

Lieberman packed the components in cotton wool,

placed them, along with the drawings, in a leather
attaché case. Then the two men went upstairs to
wait. Outside, it was dark again, the night pressing in
blackly on the empty windows. David paced, fatigue
dragging at him, sustained only by the tremendous
excitement of the moment.

Less than half an hour passed before the bell rang,
the agreed signal, startlingly loud. Lieberman opened
the door, admitted four ordinary-looking men in grey
business suits.

"I'm Conway, Supervisory Agent for the area," the
dapper, grey-haired man in the lead said. He flipped
open a wallet to show a card and badge, introduced
his three companions. "If you're ready, gentlemen. . . ."

David and Lieberman went down the walk flanked
by the four men, entered an unmarked black car. It
pulled from the curb, did an illegal U-turn, headed
back along the dark street.

Three blocks later, Lieberman spoke suddenly.

"We're heading away from the city; this route leads
out of town!"

"That's right, sir," Conway said easily. "We're taking you to a field office."

David looked sideways at the bland face of the
man seated on his right, turned to meet Al Lieberman's worried glance. Suddenly the physicist leaned
forward.

"Stop the car!" he ordered the driver. The man
looked over his shoulder with a mildly surprised expression, then at Conway, beside him in the front
seat.

"Is anything wrong?" The grey-haired agent inquired with lifted eyebrows.

"Stop the car!" Lieberman repeated.

"Do as he says, Jim," Conway said. The car slowed,

pulled to the curb. They were in a suburban street of small shops and row houses, dimly lit by antiquated streetlamps. Lieberman opened the door, put a foot out. No one else moved. David was watching the faces of the men. Conway nodded.

"You're concerned," he said. "You think this may be a trap." He reached to the dash, lifted a small telephone receiver with a dial mounted in the base, passed it back.

"This is radio telephone," he said. "Call anyone you like; FBI headquarters in Washington, if you wish. Set your mind at rest."

Lieberman took the instrument. The hum of a dial tone filled the car. He dialed a number, listened.

"Hello, Walter?" he said. "Al Lieberman here. Just, ah, called to ask about the conference next Monday ..." Pause. "Yes, you're right, it is Wednesday. Just wanted to check. Thanks." There was a click and the hum resumed. Lieberman let his breath out in a sigh; he handed the phone back.

"I ... I'm sorry. It was just that ... what we have here ..."

"I understand," Conway smiled briefly. "Shall we go on now?"

David leaned back, forced his tensed nerves to relax. Both he and Al were overly wrought-up, suspicious. But it was all right now. They were in good hands. The car sped smoothly past the last of the houses, past a lonely service station, out along a country road. David felt his eyes closing. In spite of the stay-awake drugs Lieberman had given him, the days and nights without sleep were catching up. ...

A rhythmic beat penetrated his half-doze. His head came up sharply, listening. The muffled whump-whump-whump seemed to be coming from overhead, approaching from off to the left. He leaned across Al

Lieberman to stare upward through the glass. Lights hung in the air a few hundred yards distant, lights which moved, pacing the car, swinging in a wide arc, slating in across the road now . . .

"Watch it!" David shouted. "The copter . . !"

There was an instant of confusion as the man at the wheel craned, hesitating; Conway's hand shot inside his coat, came out with an automatic pistol. Lieberman grabbed at Vincent's arm.

"What is it, Dave—?" In the glow of the crimson running light under the helicopter, David saw something small drop away, arcing down.

He dived foward over the seat, grabbed the wheel, wrenched it hard to the left. Tires squealed as the heavy car veered across the road, struck the shoulder in a spray of gravel, slammed his head against the doorpost. He was aware of a blinding flash of light, a spine-wrenching jolt, a momentary sense of flying through the air. Then blackness.

## CHAPTER SIX

THROUGH A RED-SHOT HAZE, David Vincent fought his way up into blurred light, pain, consciousness. Gravel cut into his cheek. He was lying face down on a rocky slope, among rank weeds. Fifty feet away, the car lay on its side, one wheel spinning lazily. Men moved there, as if searching.

There was a sharp, raucous buzz nearby. He turned his head, looked up into a harsh, angular face. The mouth was formed into a grotesque O—and from that

unnatural mouth the sound issued. An answering
buzz came from the darkness. A second man appeared beside the first. They looked enough alike to
be brothers—brothers of Security Chief Dorn. Or, no,
David corrected himself. Not brothers; one was short,
thick-set, with pale hair, the other tall, heavy-jawed,
with a glistening bald skull. They were more like
fellow members of some pasty-faced, hawk-eyed
tribe. Alike, as Orientals or Zulus are alike, not as
cousins . . .

"Stand," one of the men rasped as he saw that
David's eyes were open. As he spoke, his lips relaxed
into a more normal appearance. He stooped, caught
David roughly by the arm, lifted him to his feet as
easily as if he were a straw dummy. David staggered,
caught himself. He could feel the drugs stirring in his
blood, stimulated by the shock. All his senses seemed
suddenly preternaturally keen. He was aware of the
chorus of discordant buzzes from the three men by
the wreck, the faint groan from a dark figure laid out
beside it, the crackle of dead grasses under trampling
feet.

The iron-like hand on his arm urged him roughly
forward. The helicopter had landed fifty feet away.
Lights gleamed softly from its open door. David saw
Conway, lying crumpled near it, one leg twisted under him, a terrible wound across the side of his head,
not breathing. A second man lay a few yards distant,
on his back, eyes open, glazed. Two gone. The others—

A man was beside the car, holding something in his
hand that flickered. He tossed it in through the car's
shattered window. At once, arc-bright flames leaped
up, and against them David saw slumped figures
silhouetted—

"All" he shouted, leaped forward—and was flung to
the ground with stunning force. He struggled to hands

and knees, was again hauled upright. Then he saw the physicist, lying on the ground, two of the leather-faced men bending over him. David's captor buzzed. The men lifted Lieberman's limp body, carried it to the copter. David was propelled up behind him. Four men clambered in, silent, grim-faced. One took the controls. With a beat of rotors, the heli lifted off, swung away at tree-top level. Below, David caught a final glimpse of the car, burning fiercely.

For the next half-hour the copter raced through the night detouring at intervals around concentrations of light, never venturing above one hundred feet of altitude—a precaution, David guessed, against radar detection. Beside him, Al Lieberman lay, breathing stertorously. There was blood on his face. Two of their captors were busy with him, running instruments over his body. One buzzed to the man in the front seat beside the pilot. He replied in the same unearthly rasp. The copter dropped lower, hovered over a wooded ravine. One of the men opened the side door. Cold air blasted in. Too late, David lunged as Lieberman's body was unceremoniously, callously heaved over the side. A wild yell tore from Vincent's throat; he swung a blow that caught one of the grey-faced men full in the face—and then hands like steel claws caught him, hurled him back, and again the copter was lifting, sliding away into the night.

*All right,* David thought. *I'll wait, look for my chance. And when it comes*—But the thought would not complete itself. For against such force, what could a single man, exhausted and injured, hope to accomplish?

2

David lay slack in the seat, drifting in and out of

consciousness, only half aware of the terse, buzzing conversation of the murderous quartet around him. Hours passed. He came alert at a change in the swift motion. The heli circled, climbing steeply, rocking in an updraft, then dropping abruptly. Dark walls rose up around the machine—walls of jagged rock, topped with ranks of tall pines. There was the jar of landing, then a rush of bitter cold air as the door dropped open. Rough hands thrust him outside, hustled him impatiently across uneven, snow-patched ground toward the lights of a small shed, perched at the edge of a yawning abyss.

Inside a rough-board-walled room, one of the men pressed at a panel; it swung back. Beyond it, a featureless, grey corridor, stretched away. The air here was hot, stifling, bearing an acrid odor of sulphur.

At the end of the passage they came into a small, bare room. The ceiling glowed with a cold yellow illumination which gave David's hands the color of dead flesh. The faces of the four silent men were horror masks of colorless putty. Their mouths formed obscene O's as they buzzed their alien buzzing at each other.

The only furnishings in the room were a table and two chairs. The tallest of the four men pointed.

"Sit there."

David obeyed, feeling the dull pain in his back, the pull of drying blood across the side of his face. His eyes burned, his temples throbbed. One of the men stepped forward, placed the attaché case containing the parts and drawings of the strange machine on the table, seated himself. He sat opposite David. The other three men stood against the wall, watching with hooded, malevolent eyes.

"Where did you learn of the Eruptor?" the seated man demanded in a tone devoid of emotion.

David shook his head. He was aware of the murmur of air through a ventilator grill, the soft creak of the chair, the loud, heavy thump of his own heartbeat.

His own heartbeat—but no other. Somehow he knew the pulses of the men should have been audible to him in his unnatural state of drugged sensitivity, but only a faint whispering came from the men in the room—a soft susurration, like a teapot about to boil. David felt a stab of utter cold inside him—a sensation as if he had thrown back the blankets of his bed and uncovered a coiled, somnolent rattler....

"You will answer my questions," the inquisitor said. "If you resist or lie, there will be pain." His hand shot out, caught David's wrist, squeezed; agony shot up his arm. He gasped, almost fell forward onto the table.

"Who told you of the Eruptor?" the man repeated.

"No ... nobody ..." David gasped out. In the grip of the unhuman creature he was as helpless as an infant. For a moment, rage swept through him—but he caught it, checked it. *Not yet,* a voice inside cautioned him. *Wait, and watch....*

"Was it Professor Lieberman?" the relentless voice pressed on.

"No! I went to him ... he had nothing to do with it ... until I told him ..." Why did you kill him?"

"He would have died. He was useless to us. Why did you not attempt to lie, place the blame on him? He is beyond us now."

"I'm ... telling you the truth." David's voice was a hoarse croak. His throat seemed scalded by fire. All the weariness of the past week was on him now. Only the drugs kept his mind clear, his hearing keened.

"How did you learn of the true nature of the Eruptor?"

"I figured it out . . . for myself . . ."

Pain shot up his arm. For an instant his senses swam. He was dimly aware of a blow on the side of the head as his head struck the table. A humming filled the room.

". . . . awake . . . answer my questions . . ." a remote voice echoed from somewhere far away. Then buzzes, hands that shoved him upright. Through half-closed lids he saw a door in the opposite wall open—and Dorn stepped through.

## 3

There was a moment of silence. The man at the desk rose; all four faced the newcomer. His eyes went to David as he sagged in the chair.

"What are you doing with him?" Dorn barked. One of the four started to reply in the shocking, alien buzz, but Dorn cut him off:

"Speak the native language, you fool! You'll betray us yet with your carelessness!" He stepped to David, thumbed up an eyelid. David lay slack, head lolling.

"The creature is in grave condition!" Dorn rasped. "Would you kill him before you have the information?"

David felt a sharp pain in his arm. He didn't move.

"The fatigue poison level is dangerously high," Dorn said. "Administer a hypnotic and allow him five hours' dormancy. Then rouse him and drain him dry." David saw the false Security man turn on the one who had begun the questioning. "This one represents a flaw in our concealment—perhaps a traitor among us—a mortal danger. If you allow him to die ..." He left the threat hanging in the air.

David pretended unconsciousness as ungentle hands clutched him, carried him through the door, down steps, along a corridor, through echoing rooms. Suddenly light glared in his face, through his closed eyelids; abruptly he was deposited on a hard cot, felt a rough blanket tossed carelessly over him. There was a sudden, acrid odor as a cold mist stung his face. Then the light winked out, a door thudded. Cautiously, he opened his eyes.

He was alone.

4

The room was small, blank walled, dusty, lit by a faint glow from the ceiling. David prowled, found no opening in the seamless plastic partitions other than the door through which he had entered, now rigidly locked. There was a small hole in the jamb, six inches from the closed panel. He searched his clothes for something—anything—with which to probe. His pockets were empty. Then at a sudden thought he checked the collar of his grimy shirt. There was a wire stiffener, stitched inside the cloth. A moment later, he had worked it free, straightened it. Carefully, he inserted it in the aperture. There was a soft click and the panel slid back.

The dim-lit corridor was empty. Off to the right, David heard faint voices. He went that way, approached the entry to a large room. From concealment, he looked in at tables, shelves stacked with papers, a man, his back toward David, seated before a rank of TV screens, all dark and silent—except one. Pale light danced across it—the hazy, wavering outline of a narrow, unsmiling face—a member of the Tribe.

"... brood racks cannot long endure the null-G condition," a flat voice was whispering. "Nutrient supplies approach exhaustion; energy flow levels dropping rapidly. Contact must be made within one half revolution ..."

"You have already been informed that no further support is possible!" the seated man replied coldly. "Repeat, no support possible! You must wait—until the cloud passes!"

"We have passed outside contact range. Now in planetary shadow at hundred minute level. *Ornyx* supplies at minimal level; shielding failure rate 9. The unit requires immediate extrapolative vector of grade 7—"

"Revert to secondary plan! Recommend immediate disposal of twenty percent of stasis pods! Reset guidance complex to self-programming! The survival-probability balance is at equity, trending negative! Repeat, trending negative! You are now on self-supportive basis. Attempt no further contact!" As the incomprehensible voices droned David retreated, passed the door to the room where he had been confined, went on to the end of the passage. A narrow stair led upward. As he started up it, he stumbled, went down. The hypnotic administered by his captors dragged at him. But he fought it, fought the accumulated fatigue—and went on, his head filled with a relentless humming. A hot mist seemed to float behind his eyes.

He passed a landing, went up another short flight, through a door into a corridor like the one below. There was a door at the end of the hall. He started for it, caroming off the wall as his exhausted legs almost failed to carry his weight. David reached the door, paused to listen. Silence. He pushed the panel back, looked inside. His sense of direction hadn't failed him. It was the room where he had been interogated. There was the table, with its two empty chairs—and spread out on the table-top, the components of the device Dorn had called the Eruptor.

David groped for a chair, half fell into it. With a terrible effort, he forced his mind to clarity, focussed his eyes on the parts laid out before him. He remembered the sketches, his own and Al Lieberman's reconstruction of the proper assembly of the infernal machine. The red wafer first, fitted atop the blue egg-shape, the leads snapping into position here, and here. . . Then the fancifully wrought grip, sliding under to lock in place, welded as firmly as if it had been forced in one piece with the rest. And last, the assembly that he and Lieberman had constructed in the basement shop. The rods fitting snugly into matched sockets; the heavy leads slid in place, one to each side. The axial member eased home, and twisted tight—

A tingle flowed through David's hand, like a sharp electrical shock. From the coil atop the disruptor, an eerie nimbus of light sprang up, leaped in a crackling violet spark to the vertical rod at the end of the 'barrel.' There was a sharp ping, as of contracting metal. Then the Disruptor lay on his palm, inert, deadly—waiting.

At that moment, feet sounded near at hand; the door slammed wide. One of *them* stood there, his clay-like face a mask of cold fury. In a step, he reached the table, stretched out a long arm—

David brought the weapon up, his thumb stroked the firing stud. Instantly, with a sharp crackling, like dry wood in a fire, a pencil-thin beam of cold green light lanced out, impaled the alien. David hurled himself aside and the other crashed into the table, smashing it into kindling as he hurtled on across the room, slammed the opposite wall, rebounded, fell like a thing of broken wires to the floor. From a ragged hole in the victim's chest a curl of smoke came, nothing more. Not a drop of blood marked the awful wound.

Then, as David took a halting step forward, sudden, searing pain scorched his hand. With a muffled grunt of agony, he dropped the Eruptor. It was suddenly scorching, searing hot! As he watched, it glowed a dull red, then faded back into its normal, incongruous carnival colors.

Now other feet clumped in the corridor. There was a door at David's back. He whirled through it, sprinting for the entry through which he had been brought, reached the camouflaged door, burst through it, on through the outer door, and was outside, under a stark, starry sky, circled by a rim of rock. Icy wind plucked at him, sucking the heat from him, freezing his breath in his throat. He couldn't stay here, unprotected, in what felt like sub-zero weather. The dark shape of a larger building loomed nearby, he ran for it, skirting the sheer drop-off in the center of the crater-like hollow, pushed past the sagging edge of the broken barn door—and was in an echoing chamber, concrete floored. Filtering starlight showed him stacked cases, high piled crates, drums, bags. It was a storeroom, bulging with supplies. David ducked into a pitch-dark aisle, thrust his way all the way back to the wall. He could go no further.

## CHAPTER SEVEN

OUTSIDE, A VOICE CALLED—a shrill cry, like the scream of some great bird of prey. Using what seemed the last of his strength, David reached, found a grip, pulled himself up the top of the stack of cases, lay flat, twelve feet above the floor. Across the wide room, the outer door opened, and three men came in.

Hardly breathing, David watched them come, moving cautiously along the aisle, the rays of powerful handlights flicking ahead.

"The creature cannot have gone far," Dorn's voice said. "The data on their capacities for endurance show that he has been pressed far beyond the normal collapse-point—"

"The data are flawed," another cut in harshly. "I think many of our data are flawed. Already the survival probability has fallen to unity."

"Impossible!" Dorn snapped. "AGAINST THESE PUNY" "Against these puny beings the Great Race must prevail!"

"Then why do four of us hold this station alone, waiting still for the relief pod—"

"It is your duty to carry out the commands of the Survival-master—not to question them!" Dorn's voice was a cold raging. "Now find this sick weak animal! On that all our fates hinge—and the fates of broods yet unformed! You—take that side! And you, the other!"

The reply was a harsh, contemptuous buzz—but

the two ... creatures; David could no longer think of them as men—moved off, while Dorn lingered near the door.

For the next fifteen minutes—a quarter of an hour that seemed like an eternity—the *things* prowled below, poking into every cranny among the heaps and stacks of materiel.

"Not here," one called flatly, emotionlessly.

"Nor here," the other reported.

"Then," Dorn said, "he must be ..." his voice broke off, switched to the buzzing language. Now his time had run out, David knew. It would be only a matter of seconds now before the probing lights swept across his hiding place, exposing him. He came to all fours, moved softly forward. The three moved along the aisle, buzzing softly to each other. They were between David and the door. There was no escape—and he had had enough experience of their monstrous strength to retain no illusions as to the outcome of a hand-to-hand fight....

But if he could enlist some weapon—any weapon. Anything other than his bare hands. But there was nothing: only the massive, smooth-surfaced cases on which he crouched.

*Massive.* The word caught at his mind, and with it a picture. There might be a chance—a slim chance—but it was worth a try.

David felt over the surface of the crate beneath him, found the corners. He gripped it, heaved with all his strength. It barely stirred. No good. He had to find one in a better position, one he could get a full-handed grasp on. Through the gloom, he made out the shape of a lone box, perched above the rest. He went across to it soundlessly. It was even bigger than the others, smooth, with almost a soapy feel under his hands. He braced himself, pushed. The heavy crate budged, moved a foot nearer the edge. Getting a new purchase, David lunged again against the ponderous weight, slid it across another yard. And another. And now it was poised on the edge.

He looked below. Dorn was posted by the door again, something glinting in his hand. The other two approached, one carrying a light ladder. It was too late now to change the position of the crate. David could only wait, hoping for his chance.

The two men had stopped ten feet away, erected the ladder against the crates. One stepped up on it, paused to shift his light to the other hand. David shifted his position to place himself behind the crate, concealed from the ladder. A moment later a head appeared, shoulders. The climber pulled himself up, flashed his light past David's hiding place—then turned, went the other way. David risked a look below. The one on the ground turned, scanning the darkness across the way, then—as David's heart seemed to skip a beat—took a step forward. And another. And another. One more—

Dorn's harsh voice called out, and the man above answered, "Nothing here."

David braced his feet, his hands gripping the crate, waiting. . . The creature below paused, hesitated— then took his last step, and David heaved with all the remaining strength of his body. The crate resisted for a moment, then slid smoothly forward, over the edge—

The impact was a dull boom like the muffled explosion of a bomb. Even before the first echo had died. David was up, racing for the far end of the big shed. Behind him he heard Dorn's shout, the strangled croak of the victim, saw the slashing beam of the handlight playing across the spot he had occupied a moment before.

He reached the end wall. No escape here. To the

right, the stack of crates dropped sheer to the dark floor—and there in the darkness, something bulked. A stray ray of light from the far end of the room fell across it. It was a fork-lift, used for moving the stock. In an instant, David had dropped down, was beside the machine, his hands exploring the controls. It was a familiar type, one he could have disassembled and reassembled in the dark. Silently, he eased into the operator's seat. There was no time now to calculate odds, plan strategy. His one possible ally was the element of surprise. His feet found the pedals, his hand touched the starting button, pressed it. With a blattering roar, the powerful engine burst into life. David flipped the headlight switch, and the brilliant beams burned down the length of the long room, outlined the fallen crate, canted at an awkward angle, by the broken body pinned beneath it, the two figures who bent over it, straightening now, staring. . . .

David slammed the vehicle in gear, yanked the throttle lever full down. The big wheels surged and spun; the fork-lift leaped forward. David steered straight for the doors, crouched behind the partial shield of the lifting mechanism. He passed the crate, caught a glimpse of a body folded backwards, the head, blind eyes bulging, jammed between the twisted ankles. . .

There was a flicker of motion ahead, a flash of light. David ducked, and a livid blue beam hummed past him. He saw his attacker, braced against the closed doors ahead, taking careful aim for the killing shot. There was no evasive action open to him, no place to hide. He gritted his teeth, dropped beneath the wheel, steering straight for the door—

A harsh hum, a glare, a shower of sparks, a spatter of molten metal—and then a shock—a rending and smashing, a numbing blow on the shoulder that knocked him from his seat. He fell clear, struck and rolled, saw the fork lift, one head-light blazing like a fierce eye, blunder on into the sub-Arctic night, the dangling body of the gunman transfixed on the out-thrust tine.

3

David came to his feet—and Dorn's flat voice rang out from the shadows:

"Stop there! I offer you your life—for information—"

David spun, sprinted for the cover of tumbled rocks. Behind him he heard the ripping crackle of the Eruptor. Ahead, vivid light glared, cutting through a great boulder like a knife through cheese as the ravenous beam annihilated the matter in its path.

And then a hoarse howl of agony, a scream that seemed it must rip open the throat it came from. David dived flat, spun to see Dorn whirl, throw the Eruptor from him. It arced high, glowing as bright as a phosphorus flare, dropped down at the edge of the central pit—bounced high, and disappeared into the depths.

For a moment David lay where he was, gasping for breath. Far away, something rumbled dimly. He felt a faint vibration through the rock beneath him, then a harder shock. A continuous, crashing hiss started up, coming from the dark chasm where the Eruptor had fallen. Light glared then abruptly, lighting the tree-tops. Even here, fifty yards distant, the heat was like a physical blow. David staggered to his feet, saw the tall, lean figure of Dorn, gripping his burned hand in agony, outlined against the glare as he ran for cover. Driven by the intense heat, David backed, retreating up the slope as the glow increased.

Now he could see what looked like a lake of fire, rising in the white-hot throat of what David now saw was an old volcanic crater. Choking fumes rose, were whirled away by the wind. The magma reached the rim of the inner bore, spilled over, spreading to engulf the fork-lift, then the warehouse, broaching the door to the tunnel complex, pouring inside. The trees flared up like giant torches as the molten rock reached them.

From the shelter of a point of rock high above, David watched while the boiling hell of energy below spread out among the blackened trees, crept away in crimson fingers among the rocks, remembering Al Lieberman's fears of a self-sustaining sub-nuclear reaction that would consume any matter in its range, raging on without end. . . .

But at length the glow diminished, the heat waned. In an hour only a hundred-foot pool of dull-glowing lava marked the position of the vanished installation. Then he slumped where he sat and sank down into bottomless sleep.

4

He awoke staring at a ceiling papered with a pattern of pink flowers. Painfully, he turned his head, saw the smiling countenance of an elderly woman in nurse's costume, beyond her the heavy, stolid features of a State Policeman.

"Only a few minutes, Doctor said," the woman said softly, and withdrew.

"We saw the eruption," The policeman frowned, shook his head in perplexity. "Lucky for you; you were more dead than alive, Mr. Vincent. I guess you were the only one that got clear." He shook his head. "Too bad. All those scientists—all that equipment. I

helped them set up the research station just last fall."
He looked at David sharply. "Don't remember seeing
you before. . ."

David thought over his answer quickly, decided
against blurting the facts." I was new there," he said.
"Just arrived. You said—nobody got clear?"

The cop nodded thoughtfully. "Some tracks in the
snow—thought for a while one might have made it.
But the trail ended up slope on bare rock. Nobody
there." He clucked sympathetically.

The nurse had left the room now. The cop leaned
closer. "It's OK, Mr. Vincent;" he said conspiratorial-
ly. "I got a call from the FBI after I sent out my
tracer on you. The other fellow's in bad shape, but
they say he'll live. Dr. Lieberman, I mean. What is it,
a kidnaping ring? They must have worked him over
good. Amnesia, they said. Remembers nothing since
about two weeks ago. Blanked out."

"Al's all right?" David felt a surge of relief.

"Sure. But all four of the FBI boys were dead.
Tough. I don't guess you got a look at the killers'
faces . . ?"

For the next half hour, the cop went on with his
questions, supplying most of the answers himself—it
was plain that the authorities knew nothing of the
real nature of the disaster.

For two days, David rested in the small nursing
home, located, he was told, in a small town in
Wisconsin. On his feet again, wearing stiff, new
clothes bought at the local emporium, he went to a
pay phone, called the home office of MID-20th.

"Mr. Vincent!" the voice of Miss Clay, the executive secretary gasped. "We heard you'd been in an
accident. . . !"

"I'm all right," David said. "Let me talk to the
General." He had made the decision while he still lay

in the hard, starched bed. There was no point in reporting the fantastic thing he had uncovered direct to the police, or even the FBI or CIA. The only proof had been the strange weapon—the Eruptor. And that was gone now, lost at the core of the volcano it had stirred to new life. But if General Moore would believe him—and place the vast resources of MID-20th at his disposal—

"But—Mr. Vincent," the woman's strained voice came back. "You mean—you haven't heard. . . ?"

Coldness gripped David's chest. Abruptly, the artificial sense of safety about him shattered; he felt again the icy awareness of danger, close and deadly.

"Heard what?"

"The General—he's dead. He was killed ten days ago, in an automobile accident. . . ."

In a half-daze, David hung up the phone, Out in the bright street, he looked about warily, sensing a threat in every shadowy doorway, every blind, curtained window.

He knew about them. Only he, of all Earth's millions. Even Al had had the memory driven from his mind by the terrible experiences he had undergone. But they were here; they were real. The Invaders.

For that was what they were, David knew with a chilling certainty. Invaders, being, not human, not of this Earth. Here, among humanity, infiltrating the society of their victims, working, planning, toward—what?

He didn't know. But the knowledge that they existed was enough to start with. Perhaps they thought him dead, killed in the destruction of the hidden station. Perhaps that was his ace-in-the-hole. Because he was alive, with the knowledge of their existence. But not enough knowledge, not yet.

But he could get more. Thank God for the healthy

balance in his bank account. It would keep him for a while—a year, perhaps if he were careful. He couldn't risk returning to his home, his job—if it still existed. He would have to work alone, in secret, to ferret out some irrefutable proof of the terrible truth. From now on—from this moment until the day of success—that would be his mission.

Alone, David walked away down the empty street, bearing the burden of his knowledge.

**PART TWO —** *THE MANIAC*

### CHAPTER ONE

FROM HIS SEAT in the cramped corner booth in the down-at heels diner, David Vincent studied the customers seated at the zinc-topped counter: a burly truck driver in a scuffed leather jacket, a small, rabbit-faced man in overalls and mackinaw, a thin, tired-looking woman with colorless hair, lighting her third cigaret in less than five minutes with fingers that shook as she held the match. Not a savory dinner crowd—but human enough, David decided. As was the tallowy, thick-fingered woman behind the counter, and the old man at the table near the door, sipping a cup of coffee held in both hands to warm them. Outside, beyond the streaked, neon-festooned window, the night pressed close. It had been three months since David's life had been turned upside down by the discovery of the creatures he had come to think of as the Invaders. Three months since he had dropped out of sight, leaving his job, his home, his friends. Three months of wandering, never sleeping two nights in the same place, ever on the alert, avoiding all close human contacts, always watching, watching, for any clue, any evidence of the workings of the fantastic plot that he—and he alone—suspected.

The waitress—a slim, auburn-haired girl whose pert face bore only a faint resemblance to that of the obese short-order cook, doubtless her mother—placed a plate in front of him.

"More coffee?" she invited. Her brown eyes tried to hold his; her lips held a smile ready. But he glanced away, muttered a surly "No."

"I ... hope the eggs are the way you like them," the girl persisted.

"Yeah," David growled, and lifted his folded newspaper, made a show of reading it. He looked after the girl as she walked away.

*Sorry,* he thought after her. *But I can't risk involving anyone—even by exchanging a friendly word. Because I never know who—or what—might be watching....*

A line in the newspaper caught his eye:

SAUCER CULTISTS TO REVEAL 'PROOF'

David read on:

> There are aliens among us—or so at least the dedicated members of Waynetown's Interplanetary Surveillance and Interpretive Society believe. And tonight, at a special meeting of the group's members at Society headquarters in the former City Opera House, they will produce evidence to support their contention. Mr. Alphonse Cabrito, President of the UFO-watching organization announced today that new data uncovered only this week will convert thousands of sceptics to acceptance of what he refers to as 'the obvious'. "To anyone observing the present state of

human affairs," Cabrito stated in an ex-
clusive interview, "it's plain that malig-
nant alien forces are at work. . ."

There was more, written in the same tongue-in-
cheek style, enlarging on the activities of the cultists,
milking the material for laughs, as was usual. But
David's smile was more bitter than amused. News
items like this appeared in every paper in the country, practically daily. If the Invaders had set out to
create a climate of public scepticism as a cover for
their activities, they couldn't have picked a more
effective method. . . .

. . . *if they had set out to create a cover for their
activities.* . . .

It was a possibility, the thought flashed in David's
mind. Even if the Invaders had not themselves in-
vented the UFO fad, they might still have seen the
possibilities in it, seized upon the opportunity, gone
on to lend support to saucer groups, supply mislead-
ing hints, even afford glimpses of genuinely alien
artifacts or phenomena to selected dupes—or organizations. This organization—ISIS as it was referred to
in the article—for example. And if so, perhaps there
would be an alien representative at tonight's meeting,
hovering somewhere in the background, keeping an
eye on things.

—And even if there weren't, David checked his
sudden enthusiasm, it would be interesting to see
what the "proof" consisted of. The article had said the
meeting was open to the public. He would go, mingle
with the credulous, and keep his eyes open. Maybe—
with luck—and it was time for a little luck—he would
see something that would give him a new lead into
the terrible mystery that had darkened his life.

2

A knot of people stood on the sidewalk under the sagging marquee, with its rows of dusty, lightless bulbs still spelling out the name of some vanished farce of a forgotten year. A few new posters with lettering amateurishly scrawled in garish color announcing the ISIS meeting were tacked to the warped wooden frames of display boards, covering tattered playbills bleached by time. In the dusty ticket booth, a plump woman in a fantastic hat fussed with a roll of tickets, her eyes darting out hopefully at the sparse passersby.

As David Vincent paid off his cab, the group before the old opera house eyed him silently, watched as he bought his ticket, declining the literature pressed on him by the plump woman.

"Just any contribution you care to make," she squeaked. "But you *must* read of Swami Ramchandra's latest psychic energization methods," her bleating voice followed him as he turned away. A tall, angular woman with a determined chin and severe tweed skirts blocked his path.

"I see that you're not the sort to be misled by any of that heathen hocus-pocus," she stated in a flat midwestern twang, her coal-black eyes darting past David to impale the plump woman. "This is a matter for modern science, not some greasy foreigner with a towel on his head. Now. . ." She unsnapped a handbag as big as an overnight case, drew out a pamphlet. "My departed husband perhaps you've heard of him, Creely, Doctor M. Creely, not a medical doctor actually, his certificate was from the East Indiana Academy of Manufrictional Sciences, was at the time of his death working on his Manifestor, and it's been my privilege to carry on his work, inspired directly, of course, by his post mortem communications—"

"Excuse me," David edged past her, made six yards before being cornered by a tiny, spidery man with a sparse goatee, old fashioned *pince-nez*, a tarnished frock coat. He held up a veined hand; David was forced to stop to avoid bowling the little man over.

"My boy, have you heard the word?" the old gentleman demanded in a quavering tone.

"Yes, indeed, sir," David came back promptly. "Orthofoniationality."

"How's that?" the little man's eyes narrowed. "Who told you?"

"Deduction; sheer deduction. Now, if you don't mind—"

"A wise punk," the old man snarled, his voice suddenly gravelly. "If I was a couple years younger, I'd break your jaw!"

"Why, Professor Wisdom," a shocked female voice cut in. David turned, almost choking on a dense cloud of perfume. A strapping blonde girl, at least six feet one in height, fluttered eyelashes at the tiny man, took David's arm possessively. Her long hair swirled as she shook her head reprovingly at the peppery professor. "You mustn't be rude to our new friends... must he?" she inquired in a cooing tone, turning immense, pale blue eyes on David.

"Maybe he's got the right idea," David said. "I think I'm in the wrong place—"

"But you came to hear Alphonse—to hear about the positively incredible vibrations he picked up last night on his orgone tube oscillator..."

"My mistake," David disengaged his arm from her grip, only to have her latch on to his wrist.

"Now, now, naughty boy, you mustn't run away now, before you've even *seen*—"

"I was looking for the Shriners' Convention," David said firmly, and pried her hand loose. "It must be in the next block over." The big blue eyes stared after him aggrievedly as he turned—and locked eyes with a neatly dressed, middle-aged man, standing quietly by the wall, smoking a pipe. At once, the man lifted his eyebrows, tilted his head minutely, inviting David to his side.

"You're not one of these nuts," the man murmured as David came up. "I saw that at once." He appeared to be an ordinary citizen of about fifty, with the well-tended hands of an office worker. Only about his pale blue eyes was there a hint of tension, a look of wariness, well-concealed.

"Are you here to listen to Mr. Cabarito's disclosures?" he said in a neutral tone. As David hesitated he went on: "Cabrito is a fool and a charlatan. He looks on all this as an easy way of making a living."

"Is there any money in it?"

"The old dragon, Mrs. Creel: she's worth half a million dollars. The plump one is good for nearly as much. They're the big contributors. Cabrito keeps them at each other's throats—keeps the bidding up, you know, for honors as leading patroness." The man's mouth quirked in a brief smile.

"I take it you're not a Believer?" David asked.

The man's lip twitched. "Do I look like an idiot? Of course I see through this transparent sham. But. . ." his eyes were wary. "There just may be something behind all this nonsense, some true *raison d'etre* for the ISIS group—and others like it."

"What would that be?" David asked innocently.

"It's a cover—or it could be. Don't mistake me; I'm

no fanatic, leaping at shadows. But the idea has occurred to me: suppose someone—or some organization—were responsible for the things which have been observed lately, all over the country—all over the world, for that matter? Things which they wanted to conceal. How better to hide themselves than behind a screen of ridicule, eh?"

"Interesting idea," David said. "What do you suppose is being hidden?" As he spoke, he kept his eyes on the saucerites milling in the dingy lobby, which was beginning to fill now as the hour for the featured event grew close.

"I'm guessing, of course," the man said. "But the thing is too big for any single individual or private organization to be behind it. And our government would hardly be likely to conduct experiments in France, for example, where numerous sightings have occurred. The same holds true for other governments. And the fact that the phenomena have been seen near large cities, including Washington, also discredits that idea. We're left with the assumption that some other power—perhaps not of this planet—is involved. That, or mass hallucination on a grand scale."

"You're assuming that the sightings are real."

"I'm assuming nothing! But *some*thing has caused hundreds, perhaps thousands, of sober, stable individuals to risk their jobs, their reputations, to report *some*thing! As to what it might be—that, sir, is what I'd like to know. Which brings me here, to meetings such as this!"

"And instead—you meet ... these." David shook his head, glancing at the wild-eyed bearded, floppy-hatted, unhappy people, misfits all, each intent, it seemed, on gaining some miniscule measure of support for a favorite theory, to sell some dog-eared

pamphlet, to solve all the world's ills in one magic
moment of conversion.

"Yes. Dreadful people. But—you're not leaving?" he
said, as David moved away. "You *must* stay! If a few
sane, responsible people like you and myself don't
attend these gatherings, monitor the proceedings—
that means that they—whoever they might be—will
succeed by default!"

"They?" David raised an eyebrow.

"Very well," the man half-smiled, shrugged. "At the
risk of sounding melodramatic, I'll call them ... the
Invaders ..." His eyes flicked to David's. For an instant they held an unreadable expression; then they
became remote, opaque. "If they're here," he went on
softly, "if this *is* a cover for their activities—I for one
intend to learn what I can of them. Are you with
me?"

"All right," David said, feeling the tension stir inside him. "I'll see it through."

## CHAPTER TWO

INSIDE THE GLOOMY, ornate hall, inadequately lighted
by yellowed luminaires spaced along the cracked,
stuccoed walls, David and his new acquaintance—
Winifer Thrall, as he had introduced himself—took
seats in the first row, flanked by a lean, anxious-
looking man with hollow cheeks and lank grey hair,
and a portly Chinese gentleman, perspiring heavily in
a thick wool suit.

"No good sitting in the rear," Thrall whispered.

"Can't make out the trickery from there."

"What trickery?" the Chinese stared accusingly at the man. "Is that all you're here for, Jack, to find fault?"

"I wasn't addressing you, sir," Thrall said smoothly "My friend and I—"

"What you bums need is a set of Madame Chow's guaranteed lucky joss sticks," the Oriental continued, leaning to one side so as to extract a box from his side pocket. "Now, it just happens I got a spare set on hand. Tell your fortune, bring you success in your work, deliver the girl of your dreams, a steal at ..." his darting shoebutton eyes assessed David's wardrobe. "—a buck fifty. Apiece," he added, noticing that the clothes, though worn, were of expensive cut.

"Please—save your superstitious nonsense for someone else," Thrall hissed as the moth-eaten curtain across the stage twitched. A feeble spotlight winked on, hunted across warped floorboards, glinted from the toes of a pair of shoes showing under the curtain. The light moved up as the drapes parted; a woman stepped through, squinting against the glare. It was the horsey dowager with the heavy tweeds, David saw Mrs. Creel. She waited while a patter of applause died down, then in a penetrating voice said, "Fellow Isisians, guests, and yes, even the merely curious. You too are welcome, as are all who come to hear the inspired words of our enlightened leader, that clear-seeing prophet of the stirring events unfolding in our time, Mr. Alphonse Cabrito!"

There was another spattering of handclaps as the woman turned, plucked at the curtain, became entangled in its musty folds, failed to see the preternaturally lean man who stepped through the opening, blinking owlishly both ways. At that moment the woman freed herself, only to collide with the featured speaker. The stand-mounted microphone toppled, fell with a resounding clatter. The two bumped heads bending to retrieve it. Cabrito looked definitely annoyed as the woman fought her way back through the curtain, leaving the stage to him.

"Tonight," he said, blinking rapidly as he spoke in a high-pitched, nasal voice, "I have for you a demonstration which will bring the world of so-called science to its knees, begging and pleading for just one little look at the material I have uncovered in my researches during the past months—months of hardship during which I labored day and night in my privately maintained physical research laboratories—the only privately endowed research institution in America, I might add, with the sole exception of the Richmond Institute of Red Owl, Pennsylvania, unless it has at last been hounded from existence by the secret government agencies devoted to the extermination of truth in this country..."

As the thin, fanatical voice droned on, David surreptitiously studied the faces around him. There were old people, young people, men bearded and smooth-faced pretty girls, withered beldames, Nordics, Negroes, Italians; faces of every description, a truly integrated assemblage. But nowhere did he see the leathery skin, the pale, intent eyes, the curiously lifeless visages which he had come to associate with the Invaders. Neurotics, gullible sensation-seekers these might be—but aliens, no. It appeared, he thought ruefully, that the experiment was a failure. . . .

"Did you catch that?" Thrall whispered, touching David's arm. "Watch . . . he'll do it again . . ."

"Do what?"

"I didn't want to say earlier, until I was sure— but there's no mistaking it. Look!" Thrall's fingers tightened on David's sleeve. "Watch his eyes! The blinking—it's a code!"

The speaker's lids, as David had already noted, flickered incessantly as he talked. Blink-blink-blink, pause; blink-blink-blink-blink, pause, blink-blink. Cabrito's eyes closed momentarily, resumed their fluttering.

"Did you catch that?" Thrall whispered. "That was the dash. It's Morse code, or something close to it. Now, if we can just spot the one he's signalling to ..." Thrall turned, craning his neck toward the rear of the hall. Abruptly, his fingers dug into David's arm.

There—!"

David turned. A tall, narrow-faced man moved catlike across the back of the long room, disappeared through a side door. David caught only a quick glimpse of the black-browed face. Not enough to be sure, he reminded himself as his muscles tensed involuntarily in instinctive response to the deadly threat implicit in the situation. But in the dim light, the face he had seen could have been that of the man called Dorn.

"Where does that door lead?" David hissed the question.

"Backstage," Thrall replied.

"Come on." David rose; as Thrall started up, a hand caught his arm. The bland Chinese face turned up, catching the reflected light from the stage. Sweat glistened on the man's meaty features.

"Sit down, pal," he whispered. "You want to disturb the speaker?"

Thrall tugged, staring about him in distress. People's heads turned. Someone hissed "Quiet!"

David took a step, caught the Oriental's arm just below the elbow, applied pressure to a nerve. The man jerked his hand back with a muffled yelp; Thrall sprang away. The front-row viewers muttered as the two walked quickly past them.

"Through here!" Thrall led the way under a Moorish arch into a curved, stuccoed passage, past a chipped, waterless drinking fountain, up worn carpeted steps which twisted around an abrupt bend. He pushed open a paint-chipped door; over his shoulder David saw warped flied, hanging ropes, dusty props, waiting in the gloom.

"He's got to be here somewhere," Thrall hissed. "You check this side; I'll look over there." He darted away. David stood where he was in the shadowy entry, listening. Beyond the curtain, hanging in heavy folds on the left, Alphonse Cabrito's voice piped on, the words indistinct. From somewhere ahead, a soft sound came, as if something light were being dragged. . . .

David took a step—and checked as a faint pop sounded from above. He looked up—and threw himself back as something dark and silent hurtled down from the jungle-growth of ropes, slammed the ancient stage with an echoing crash. Ropes clattered down after the fallen boom; the curtain trembled, flicked open. Cabrito's petulant face appeared, turned toward David, past him. The angry eyes opened wide; the pursed lips parted—

There was a muffled sound of impact. Cabrito clutched at the curtain, staggered, fell backward out of sight. But in the moment before he vanished, David saw the sudden gush of crimson across the narrow chest. A moment later pandemonium broke out beyond the curtain.

Thrall reappeared, started as he saw David.

"What . . ? he gasped. "I thought—"

"We've got to get out of here, fast," David said quickly. "Which way?"

Thrall hesitated a moment, then he jerked his head.

"Through here." He brushed past David, lifted aside a cardboard cut-out of a giant flower pot, opened a small door onto a narrow alley. They walked along to the street, heard a siren approaching as they skirted a small coupe at the curb, crossed the street.

"My car," Thrall indicated a well-polished sedan half-way up the block. "You'd better come along to my place. There are some things I want to show you."

David looked across at the average-man face, set in an expression of sober concern. Behind the pale eyes, the wariness was more pronounced now.

"All right, Mr. Thrall, he said. "I'll be glad to see what you have to show me."

For an instant, it was as if fire flashed in the depths of Thrall's eyes. Then he nodded, opened the car door.

"Good. Let's be going before they cordon off the block."

## CHAPTER THREE

THRALL DROVE SILENTLY, through the chill, empty streets of the town. Gaunt, leafless trees stood like silent guards along the route. They pased the last of the shops, followed a winding, hedge-lined avenue past vast, ancient mansions like abandoned funeral homes.

"Gatewood Heights," Thrall said with a hint of

pride. "Finest section of town. My family has lived here since the eighties. Only myself left now, of course." He pointed. "That's Thrall House, there at the top of the rise." David saw the high gaunt outline silhouetted against the dim luminosity of the sky. A single light burned, high up in one Victorian tower.

Thrall turned in between stone posts, followed a gravelled drive, pocked with washouts; rank weeds whipped against the underside of the car. He halted before a wide porte cochere from which a rotted gutter hung down in a sagging arc.

"The place needs a little maintenance," he said briskly as he stepped out. "My researches consume so much of my time that I haven't given it the attention I should have . . ."

David got out of the car, stood looking up at the looming, dapboard front, vine-grown, the paint cracked and peeling. Thrall led the way to the wide steps. At the top he halted, fussing with bunched keys—

The sound of breaking wood warned David; he leaped back as the step on which he had started to put his weight collapsed, the tread dropping out of sight, down through a black opening. The echo told him of great depths below.

"Oh—perhaps I should have warned you, Mr. Vincent," Thrall said. "Some of these old timbers are somewhat rotten. One of those little matters I should have seen to."

"That's all right, Mr. Thrall," David said easily. "Now that I've been warned, I'll be more careful."

For a moment, their eyes locked. Then Thrall turned abruptly, opened the wide door and stepped inside.

It was a wide, high room, with water streaks on the once gaudy wallpaper, a smell of must and mould.

The furniture was massive, antique, undusted. Thrall led the way across a tarnished rug to an open double door, switched on a light—a single bulb, burning in an immense, ornate chandelier in the center of the room beyond the entrance.

"The library," Thrall said, waving a hand which took in the deep, worn leather chairs, the book-lined walls, the cold fireplace. "Why don't you have a seat here, and I'll fetch along a bottle of brandy; perhaps I could even get a small blaze going, to take the chill off the evening."

"Never mind the drink," David said. "You were going to show me something."

"Of course." Thrall flashed a shallow smile. "Perhaps you'll come along to my laboratory then."

"You're a scientist?" David asked as he followed the man to the ornate staircase which curved up to a dark gallery.

"Not in the usual sense of the word. But I've attempted to attack the problem in an orderly fashion. Organize my data, subject it to certain rigorous examinations—you understand."

"Not yet," David said. "But I'm sure you'll make it all very clear."

"I hope to," Thrall murmured. "Soon, now . . ."

They passed a landing where a jackal-headed Egyptian baxalt stared with blind, hostile eyes, started up a narrower flight. Thrall gripped the carved bannister, looking back over his shoulder.

"I hope you don't mind the climb," he called. "You'll find it easier coming down.'"

"I'm enjoying it," David said. "I have the feeling I'm getting close to something."

"You are, Mr. Vincent . . . indeed you are."

At the top, a bare, unadorned hall stretched in both directions. Thrall gestured David past him.

"After you," David said.

Thrall shot him a sharp look, brushed past, led the way along to the door at the end of the hall. He paused with his hand on the big china knob.

"Very few people have seen what lies beyond this door, Mr. Vincent," he said. "I hope you are prepared to be—shocked."

"I'm counting on it," David said. Thrall nodded curtly. "In that case . . ." He threw the door wide, reached in and flipped a switch that flooded the room with light. David stepped forward, looked past Thrall into the room—and froze at what he saw there: white tile walls, polished floor, a narrow, padded, six-foot table under a bank of fluorescents, beside it a stainless steel case of the same size, and another, smaller table, set with an array of glittering steel instruments. At one side was a panel fitted with instruments and grilles, buttons and indicator lights in rows.

"Surprised, Mr. Vincent?" Thrall said softly.

"It looks like an operating room," David said.

"I should have told you; I was trained as a surgeon—though to be sure, I've never practiced. The cartel which controls such matters saw to it that I never received my license." Thrall's voice turned harsh on the last words. "Still, I don't lack for experience—" He broke off. "But it's not that about which you wish to hear, is it, Mr. Vincent?"

"I want to hear about the aliens among us," David said flatly, watching the other's face.

"I'm afraid I wasn't completely candid with you," Thrall said. "I told you that I had deduced that if there were intruders here on this planet, they might well give themselves away through their meddling with our organizations."

David nodded. "They might."

Thrall leaned toward him. "They *have!*" he hissed.

His teeth were bared in a ferocious grin. "They were contemptuous, dismissing all Earthmen as fools— blind, credulous fools! But they were wrong, Mr. Vincent! I wasn't fooled! Not once, not by any of them! Look for yourself!" With a swift motion, Thrall tripped a lever at the foot of the steel-cased table. Like an elongated clamshell, the two halves of the cover folded back to reveal the hollow, staring eyes, the gaunt, shrunken chest, the withered legs of a long-dead man.

2

Davis held his eyes steadily on the horrid specta- cle, forcing his face to conceal his reaction to the dry brownish, flesh, the ghastly wounds where the thorax had been opened, the topless skull, sawed clean, the skeletal hand, a thing of rags and tatters.

"This is the last of them who thought himself so clever," Thrall's voice was a gloating coo now. Across the mutilated cadaver, his eyes glinted like those of a wild animal. "He came here . . ." Thrall broke off to let a titter escape from between his taut lips—"to trap *me*— in my own house, the cretin! What an opinion they must have of our intelligence, Mr. Vincent! To follow me here, into my own secret places, among my own—but there, I mustn't say too much. Suffice it to remark that in the end he learned who was mas- ter."

"You picked him up at an ISIS meeting?" David asked in a casual tone.

"Not at all. It was a convocation of the Brethren of the Celestial Light. He offered—" another chuckle "—to show me the inner significance of the constella- tions. I told him I had a private observatory—and the poor fool thought it was I who was being deluded!"

"So you killed him."

"Of course. He was a menace to my world—"

"And dissected him."

Thrall nodded. "In order to discover the anatomical differences, to aid the government in identification after I've revealed my work."

"And was he . . . an alien?"

"Of course! You think I'd have killed him otherwise?"

"How did you do it—kill him, I mean?"

"With this." Thrall's hand came from behind the case, holding a short, blued-steel revolver aimed steadily at David's chest.

"And now . . . ?" David said calmly.

"And now—it's your turn, Mr. Vincent!" Thrall leaned forward, his lips suddenly wet. "Did you imagine I wouldn't detect what you were—instantly? That you didn't give yourself away in a thousand subtle fashions? Did you really think, you blockhead, that you would be able to trick *me*?"

"Why would I want to trick you?" David asked mildly.

"You may drop the pretense now, Mr. Vincent—or whatever your real name is—Bzzkflx, or Znnqrnx, for all I know! Because I see you as you really are! I see those ghostly antlers, that fanged mouth, those leathery wings! The psychic emanation is all about you! I penetrate your disguise—!"

"What disguise?"

"The flesh-mask you're wearing! It's useless—because I know! Earth has already been invaded by aliens from a distant world! And you—you are one of Them!"

David nodded, holding the other's eyes. "I see you're too smart for us, Mr. Thrall," he said. "If we'd known the Earthmen were as brilliant as you, we'd never have tried it."

For a moment, Thrall's expression flickered. Behind the fierce smile, something else showed; something small, and frightened. Then he made a curt gesture with the gun.

"Never mind that. Now, before I kill you—I want information." Thrall paused to lick his lips, suddenly dry now. "Where do you come from? Why are you here? Were you—" He jabbed the gun at David, his expression intent. "Was it you who were responsible for my failure in medical school? Was it you who told Gwendolyn to refuse my offer of marriage? Were you the one who told my father of—" He broke off, his hand shaking. "But of course you were," he said in a voice suddenly flat. "How blind I've been. And it was you who caused my business to fail, and raised the taxes on my property, and defeated me in the race for nomination for President on the Apple Cider Vinegar ticket! And—and—"

"Not only that," David said, "we've surrounded the house. We've been watching you, Thrall—haven't you noticed?" He smiled a grim smile. "They know I'm here. They sent me here—for a purpose."

"Wha—what's that?" Thrall backed to a window, glanced quickly out. In that instant, David's hand flicked out, palmed a scalpel from the table beside him.

"Good lord!" Thrall's voice was shaky. "There's a car—hidden there, by the road . . ." He whirled on David. "But *you'll* never escape alive—"

"Wait!" David snapped. "I said I'd come for a purpose. Don't you want to hear what it was?"

"To kill me," Thrall gasped. "I'm too dangerous to you. You need to put me out of the way—"

"Nonsense," David said. "We need you. You're too

intelligent a man to kill. And your own people have never appreciated you. We want you to work for us, Mr. Thrall. You'll be made Supreme Chief Overlord of the planet as soon as it's conquered provided you cooperate with us."

"Su—supreme chief? But—you're lying It's only a trick!"

"If we'd wanted to kill you, we could have done it last week—remember?" David felt the sweat trickle down the side of his face. He was playing it by ear, from moment to moment, never knowing at what second the man across the room might snap—might begin firing wildly, pushed beyond the fragile edge that now restrained him.

"Last week?" Thrall frowned. "You mean—at the bridge?"

David nodded. "Of course."

"I thought at the time—but—"

"And the time before that," David said. "We knew you realized what was happening. We did it intentionally, let you catch a glimpse of how things were— just so that you'd realize now that killing isn't what I came for."

"But—I brought *you* here . . ."

"Did you, Mr. Thrall?" David smiled. "And I suppose you also killed Cabrito—and dropped that boom that just missed me?"

"No—of course not. But . . . that means . . . and that car down there. . . ."

"We're here in force," David said coldly. "The time has come to make your decision, Thrall! Are you with us—or would you prefer to go on fighting alone, unappreciated, despised by your own, looked down on as an eccentric—"

"No," Thrall said. His smile was a stark grimace as

he thrust the gun forward. "A failure I may be—but a traitor to my own world—never!"

The shot rang out in the same instant that David threw himself aside, slammed against the cadaver case, sending the steel box and its grisly contents hurtling across the room. A bullet spanged off metal, a second thunked solidly into wood an inch from David's head—and then Thrall screamed hoarsely as the heavy box knocked him down and backward against the dial-covered panel. David came to his feet, saw Thrall's agonized face, twisting away from contact with the outflung arm of the cadaver lying across his body.

"My . . . my legs," Thrall whispered. "You've broken them . . ."

David jumped past the stricken man to the wall switch, flipped it off. In the darkness, as Thrall whimpered, he went to the window, looked down at the weed-grown lawn, the pale ribbon of the drive leading toward the untrimmed hedge lining the road. A small, black car was parked there, amost invisible except for a stray glint of starlight from its windshield.

"Who's car is that?" David snapped.

"I thought—you said . . ."

"We both talked a lot of nonsense," David said. He lifted the heavy case off Thrall's legs, knelt to crouch beside him. "Listen to me, Thrall: I'm no Invader! I went to that meeting for the same reason you did—to get a line on them!"

"Then—you believe—they're here—among us!" Thrall's voice was a hoarse rasp of agony.

"I believe we're both in mortal danger," David said quickly. "I think we were followed here. Now—"

"But—Cabrito," Thrall said. "Didn't you—shoot him?"

"Not me—and not you! There was someone else,

Thrall! I thought at the time you were working together; but not now. You haven't killed anybody."

Thrall's eyes went to the terrible dead face of the cadaver only inches from his own, the dry lips stretched tight over yellowed teeth. "Aren't you forgetting . . . him?" he whispered.

"That's a medical supply cadaver. You can see the lesions on the underside of it from lying at the bottom of a formalin tank. Forget trying to impress me with how bad you are, Thrall! We're in trouble! And I need your help!"

"You . . . you're lying!" Thrall said with a sudden gleam of renewed fear in his eyes. "You know about last week, at the bridge—and before that, the tree . . ."

"I was stalling, stringing you along," David said. "You were holding a gun on me, remember? I had to—"

"Do your worst!" Thrall gasped out. "I'll never betray my own kind! And it's too late for your friends to help you! You'll never get out of this house alive! It's trapped, damn you! Trapped to catch Invaders! And now . . . and now . . ." His voice trailed off into a moan; his eyes rolled up and set. His head lolled sideways. David checked the injured man's pulse. It beat, weakly, fluttering.

He stood. He had been right about a couple of things—but very wrong about others. And those mistakes could be fatal. That car down below—it might be innocent enough—but it bore a remarkable resemblance to the one he had seen parked at the alley mouth, behind the Opera House. As for Thrall's warning—that might have been no more than the ravings of a demented mind. But if it were true . . .

As David turned from the window, there was a tinkle of glass, a dull *smack* of lead striking the ceil-

ing behind him. David dropped flat. There was no
guard shot; only a threatening silence.

*That answers one question,* he thought. *Now let's
see if I can get out of this place alive. . .*

## CHAPTER FOUR

At the top of the stairs, David hesitated. It was a
logical place for a trap. Thrall, he remembered, had
kept his hand firmly on the rail, hugging the left wall,
all the way up. David felt under the bannister, his
fingers touched a metal rod, countersunk in the wood,
running lengthways. He pressed it, heard a click. He
put his weight carefully on the top step. It held as he
descended.

At the floor below, he paused, listening. From somewhere, a faint sound came—or was it merely the
moan of wind under the eaves, the creak of aged
timbers? He couldn't be sure; but it would be fool-
hardy to use the main staircase; it was too exposed.
He had to find another way down.

Moving silently, David turned, went along the gallery. Near its end, something moved in the darkness.
David froze, then saw that it was only a glass-covered
picture, hanging on the wall, reflecting his face. He
started on—and Thrall's voice whispered out of the
shadows:

"Try to escape, if you will, Mr. Vincent—but you
are doomed . . . doomed . . ." The voice faded off into
a whisper. For a moment, David heard tortured
breathing; then a soft click, followed by silence.

"Hidden mikes, eh?" David murmured to himself. He wrenched the picture soundlessly from the wall. It came away trailing wires. He smiled grimly, replaced the spy-eye. Thrall was conscious again, it seemed—and following the action. Maybe in the next few minutes he'd get more than he'd counted on. . . .

The passage turned left here. David took a few cautious steps saw that it ended in a blank wall. He halted, suddenly wary, backed away—and sensed rather than heard a sliding of wood across wood. Tensed as he was, he threw himself back, as a massive panel dropped cutting off the cul de sac from which he had retreated barely in time. Thrall had not been voicing idle threats. Strangers ventured here at their own risk.

David took another turn, found himself in still another passage. He moved forward slowly, all his senses keened, his eyes straining through the darkness. There was an archway ahead. He halted, studying it, saw a small disc set in one side, emitting an almost invisible glow. Tentatively he passed a hand in front of it. Above, there was the snick of a release mechanism, and with a rush and hiss of metal on oiled rollers, a glittering blade of polished steel slammed down against the massive oak threshold with a blow that shook the floor. David stared at it with incredulous eyes. A guillotine! One more step and the infernal machine would have halved him like a melon.

Shaken, he stepped across the knee-high barrier, moved close to the wall, striving to make out detail in the faint light coming from the open window at the far end. If he could reach it, perhaps he could climb down, bypassing any other surprise the crazed man might have prepared . . .

A row of small perforations along the picture mould caught his eye. Probably they were merely nailheads, from which paintings had hung in the past, but it was as well to be cautious, here in this crazy-house of lethal snares. He reached up, touched one. The shape was a blunted cone, with a small perforation in the end; not a nail—more like a tiny nozzle—

With a sudden hiss, pale liquid jetted from the orifices. David leaped back as stinging drops of the fluid spattered his cheek and neck, burning like fire. He wiped at them with his sleeve, saw the fibres of the cloth curl and turn brown. Acrid fumes rolled along the passage—the fumes of raw sulphuric acid. Coughing, David retreated . . .

Ten minutes later, still groping through the seemingly endless maze of corridors which turned and twisted through the old house, David heard the faint click which twice before had warned him of the threat of a mechanical nightmare. This time it was impossible to tell from which direction it came. David threw himself forward, felt the swish of air by his face; a rough noose closed about his outflung arm, yanked him upright with a wrench that almost dislocated his shoulder. Hanging by one arm, with his toes barely touching the floor, David reached up, felt a harsh, hempen rope looped tight about his wrist. If his dive had taken him a few inches to the left, it would have been his neck instead of his wrist entoiled in the noose.

For a moment David hung slackly, too exhausted to struggle. And then, from somewhere ahead, a soft footfall sounded. He strained through the darkness to see, made out the vague rectangle of a stairwell. And against the lesser blackness, there was a movement. A man's head appeared, then his shoulders, coming slowly up the steps twenty feet away. For an instant, as the advancing figure passed through the faint glow from the window on the landing, his face caught the light: lean, hollow features, set in a slack, emotion-less expression—features David had seen before. The features of the alien, Dorn.

*Dorn!* the name rocketed through his mind. *Dorn, still alive—still hunting him—even as he himself hunted the Invaders.*

David tugged futilely at the rope. Then, at a sudden thought, his hand went to his jacket pocket, brought out the scalpel, he had palmed in Thrall's tower chamber of horrors. With uncertain, fumbling strokes, he slashed at the rope, felt the icy sear of pain as the blade bit into his own flesh. But he slashed again, felt tough fibres part, once more, and the rope stretched, snapped.

David landed on his feet, crouched. The dark figure on the stair had halted. David could imagine cold eyed, piercing the darkness. He didn't know how well the aliens could see in dim light. No better than he, perhaps. But this was not a time to take chances. Silently, with infinite caution, David backed away. Dorn stood where he was, his head cocked, as if listening. Somehow, that silent immobile figure was more menacing than if he had charged, howling his hatred ...

There was a railing at David's back. He recognized the spot: the gallery, above the entry hall. A few feet to the left, the grand staircase led down. From here, while hidden in deep shadow, he could see the front entry, the open library door where the light still burned feebly. Against the light, something moved, casting a long shadow across the floor. David tensed, watching as the shadow elongated. He was trapped—cornered. He moved back toward the deeper darkness near the wall—and something prodded him sharply in the back. In instant reflex, he whirled aside—and saw the basalt Death-god tilt outward, fall from its pedestal past the spot he had occupied an instant before. It struck with an impact which was deafening in the silence, smashed halfway through the floor before coming to rest amid the splintered boards.

David backed swiftly, silently, watching the darkness below. The study light snicked off, leaving total darkness. Feet sounded, crossing the floor, not bothering with caution now. They reached the steps, started up. And Dorn was advancing along the gallery now. David turned, pushed at a door behind him. It swung in—and, too late, David felt the yielding of the floor underfoot, felt himself falling headlong into blackness.

2

Even as he fell, David's hand swept out, caught the edge of the opening through which he had dropped. His groping feet scraped a rough masonry wall underlying the partition above, thumped against a parallel wall behind. The space he had dropped into was a hollow, in the walls, probably unnoticeable to anyone without a tape measure, and a previous hint of its existence. Hanging by his straining hands, David felt nothing below his feet.

Above, the steps reached the top of the stairs, hesitated, came his way. Quickly, David twisted sideways, pressed a foot against each wall—about a yard apart—and, bracing himself like a climber scaling a rock chimney, let go his handhold. He slid down a few inches; then his exploring hands found purchase. He swung against one wall, climbed swiftly down, to the floor a few feet below.

In the darkness, something rustled. "Clever, Mr. Vincent," Thrall's breathy voice hissed. "And agile as well. But it won't help you. Nothing will help you. You will die here..."

"Thrall, can you hear me—?" David whispered urgently; but the click cut off all sound. David felt his way along the narrow passage, reached a dead end. From somewhere, a cold draft blew. He heard soft sounds above, a faint humming that seemed to freeze the blood in his veins. It was a sound he had heard before; the sound of a creature not human. And now such a creature was peering down, he knew, mere feet away, searching out his hiding place...

"It is below," a cold voice said. "I monitor its air-and blood-pumps."

"Follow it," Dorn's flat voice rasped.

The reply was a harsh, inhuman buzzing.

"Speak the native dialect!" Dorn's voice was iron-hard.

"And allow the creature to overhear?"

They moved away; David heard the faint sibilance of their voices, but could no longer make out their words. He put his face close to the spot from which Thrall's voice had come.

"Thrall," he whispered. "I don't know if you can hear me; but you should know by now that I'm not the only one in the house. They're here, Thrall! They're hunting me! Listen to them! Listen to what they're saying!"

There was no reply. Had Thrall heard him? There was no way to know.

David felt over the wall. The draft had to be coming from somewhere; there must be an opening here...

He found it: a small, rectangular hatch, about eighteen inches square, probably an access hole for installation of—whatever other diabolical engines Thrall's mad mind had devised to complicate the plight of unwelcome guests. But it was a way out. As he crawled into the cramped tunnel, he heard the sound of feet scraping the walls of the space behind him.

He moved quietly along the rough planks that floored the crawlspace. There was no room to stand; splinters stung his hands and knees. Blood from the cuts on his wrist was slippery under his palm. He sensed a barrier ahead, reached out, felt bricks. The route ended here.

But the draft still flowed cold around him. He groped his way to the left, crossed open joists. An electrical cable snaked across here, incongruously massive. On impulse, David followed it, traced it to the point where it dived down suddenly to disappear through the floor. Faint light leaked in around the opening through which it passed.

He went on, twenty feet farther reached what he was sure was the outer wall of the house. With his head against the dry, dusty boards, he could feel the minute vibration from the wind outside.

Carefully, David felt his way along the wall. Behind him, at the far side of the wide, cramped crawl space, he heard soft sounds. He was no longer alone, here in the close darkness. . . .

Again rough stonework blocked his path; a chimney, he guessed. He worked his way around it—and there, set in the outer wall, his groping fingers discovered a framed opening closed by a small hinged panel and secure, by a padlock. The panel was rotted, badly fitted. It was from here that the draft came. David brushed sweat from his eyes—this in spite of the chill in the air—and gripped the door. It would be noisy, he knew, but without hesitation, he wrenched the decayed wood free, laid it aside, and thrust his head through the opening into icy, fresh air.

He was twenty feet above the ground, he saw. Starlight showed him a spiked iron fence directly below, an ornamental border for a long-defunct flower bed. It would be possible to worm through the opening, but to drop twenty feet to *that* was out of the question. There had to be another way. Leaning farther out, David scanned the wall below. There was a high window just barely in reach of his toes—perhaps—if he hung at arm's length . . .

It was not an inviting prospect—but it was the only one in sight. Swiftly he reversed himself, pushed his feet out, until he rested on his chest. Then he slid backward, forcing his shoulders through, lowering himself until his arms were extended, only his hands still grasping the frame above. He felt with his feet, found the narrow trim strip above the high window. Gingerly, he lowered his weight to it. Then, twisted sideways and pressed close against the wall, he released his grip above, bent one knee, lowering the other foot. He felt his toe slide across glass, touch a cross member. With a delicate movement, he kicked at it. The tinkle as the pane shattered seemed shockingly loud. He tested the new foothold. It seemed fragile, but perhaps it would hold. He put his weight on it, lowered the other foot—

The thin wooden var snapped, and a vivid image of the spikes below flashed through David's mind as he felt himself drop—until his hands, raking at the paint-scaled siding, caught the upper frame, held on. He found the sill under his feet. For a moment, he clung, waiting for his pulse to slow then he turned, gauging the distance below, tensing himself to jump clear.

Without warning, the casement window before him

swung in; tattered curtains billowed as the night wind swirled them. A tall, leather-face figure stood there, yellow eyes gleaming straight at David's.

"Come in, Mr. Vincent," Dorn said. "There are matters of which you and I must talk."

## CHAPTER FIVE

David stood beside the window through which he had just stepped. The feeble light of the forty wall bulb in the chandelier gleamed dully on the strangely shaped weapon in Dorn's left hand. His right, David saw, was thrust deep into the side pocket of his long coat.

"You are an elusive man, Vincent," Dorn said. Under the hard, unaccented tone, David could hear the ragged, torn-metal rasp of the alien buzz that was this pseudo-man's natural speech.

"Who wouldn't be, with you on his trail?" David said. *Spar for time*, his instinct whispered. *Wait for an opportunity . . .*

"Not many would have succeeded so well as you," Dorn said flatly. There was no flattery in his tone—or any emotion. It was a statement of fact, nothing more. "You are not like your fellow beings, Mr. Vincent. You are dangerous to me and all my kind. And yet—you might be useful, too."

"I doubt that," David said. He moved to the wall, leaned against the bookcase. His head felt light, woozy; his knees weak. Bright spots danced before his eyes.

"You have lost a considerable amount of body fluid," Dorn's voice seemed to come from far away. "Your flesh is flimsy stuff, doomed to quick death."

David fought to cling to consciousness, to hold his head up, to fight back the mist swimming before his eyes. Dimly, he was aware of the door opening, of the small, thin man who came through—or, he corrected himself, not a man: Dorn's fellow alien, an imitation of a man. . . .

Dorn's voice bored on, fading in and out. And nearer, another voice, thin and small, seemed to mingle with it. Thrall's voice.

"*Vincent . . . can you hear me? Listen. . . I heard them. . . I know now. . . you must. . .*"

David shook his head, fighting to clear it. Dorn was staring at him, his hard features rigid.

"You're sick, Vincent. I could cure you. Or I can kill you. Which is it to be?"

"You're frightened," David said, hearing his voice slur the words. "Or you wouldn't be talking . . ."

"*Keep him talking*," the tiny voice whispered, inches from his ear. "*And watch the other one. Maneuver them beneath—*"

"Stand away from the wall," Dorn rapped the command. He came forward, swept books from the shelves where David had been standing.

"Perhaps I am overly cautious," he said. "I thought perhaps you had a weapon concealed there. But you would not be so foolish."

"You want me to make a deal with you, is that it?" David said. *Keep him talking*, Thrall's voice had said. Well, it was as good a gambit as any for now. Stall him, look for a chance . . . any chance. . . ."

"I offer you life—vigor such as you have never known," Dorn said. "In return—you will perform certain small services for the Great Race."

"What services?"

"There are. . .certain areas. . .into which only a native of this small world can penetrate; certain tests we cannot pass. You will pass them for us, Mr. Vincent. You will place certain devices in specified locations, all in perfect safety. And afterwards—your reward will be commensurate with your usefulness."

"I sell out my world, is that it?" David replied. "What reward do you think you could offer me that would make that sound attractive?"

"We are skilled in the protoplasmic sciences," Dorn said. "You have seen some of our work. This body I wear is an example. I can lift a weight of one ton with a single hand, crush a steel bar in my fist, run at a speed of forty miles per hour for one hundred hours, swim miles underwater. Fire cannot harm me, nor your feeble weapons. All this—I can give to *you*, David Vincent! You will be a superman among your puny fellows! No walls can stand against you! You will have the power to take whatever you wish, money, females—"

"And if I took you up on this—how do I know I could trust you?"

"The Great Race does not lie."

"So you say."

The second alien had come forward, stood beside Dorn now.

"Kill it," he said, emotionlessly. "It will never surrender."

"I tell you this one is not like the others," Dorn rasped. "It is not a weakling, a fool! It ferreted us out, alone, alone it destroyed Station Nine, killed three of my units! It has courage, ingenuity! These are the qualities the Great Race admires! This is a man we can use!"

"Kill it," the other creature repeated.

"You see, Mr. Vincent, the pressures to which I am subjected," Dorn said tonelessly. "But if you will enter my service, voluntarily undergo the small adjustment necessary to insure your correct function—then I will sponsor you before the Survival Master himself! You will be my slave, Vincent, my property. As such, you will be safe—and all the riches of this planet will be yours to share, along with us!"

"I asked you before—how do I know I can trust you?" David temporized. Maneuver them, Thrall had been saying, just before Dorn had interrupted. Maneuver them beneath. . .

Beneath what? David's eyes scanned the room as Dorn talked on, pointing out the illogic of troubling to trick him, when it would be so easy to enslave him against this will. ". . .it is a willing slave I require, Vincent!" he declaimed. "A slave in full possession of his faculties—and of the powers, far beyond his normal capacities—that I can give him—to carry out my commands! Why should I betray you? I can kill you at any time I wish. Why should I bother to deceive you?"

"You tell me," David came back, hardly hearing the other's words. *Beneath. . .beneath. . .*His eye fell on the chandelier, a five foot diameter construction of wrought iron, weighing perhaps a quarter of a ton. And suddenly a recollection flashed across his mind: the heavy electrical cable, running across the space above. The spot where it had ended was at about the position of the chandelier. The lone-dim-glowing bulb there gave an impression of feebleness—but that cable had been heavy enough to carry a massive voltage. . . .

"I think you're lying," David said, and moved sideways, along the wall, his face registering fear, close to panic.

"Come, Vincent—I have reasoned with you, made matters clear," Dorn stated in his penetrating monotone. "You are too clever a man to throw away such an opportunity—"

"You'll turn me into a zombie, make me do your dirty work, then kill me," David blurted, and darted sideways. The creature behind Dorn leaped at him, and David spun aside, darted to the center of the room, halted facing the aliens.

"You'll have to prove you're telling the truth, prove you have the powers you claim," he said quickly, holding the aliens with his eyes. "If you do it, then I'll believe you." He backed a step; Dorn followed him, waving his companion back as he started past.

"You doubt that I can mould your body as I say, give you the strength of a lion, the steady nerves of a striking cobra? Then look!" Dorn drew his right hand from his pocket, held it up. . . .

David stared in horror at the charred stump that protruded from the cuff—the ends of the radius and ulna, burned off above the wrist, projected like sticks in a campfire, projected from the blackened, ragged flesh. And from the center of the hideous wound, like a rosebud springing from scorched earth, a tiny baby fist grew, the miniature, pink fingers stirring aimlessly.

"You see! I lost my hand—seared away by the defective Eruptor as it misfunctioned; but a new hand takes its place! In six months, there will be not even a scar to remind me of the ineptitude of your human industry in attempting to manufacture our weapons!"

"Why didn't you make them yourself?" David demanded, backing another step. "Why take the risk of farming them out to our factories?"

"It was a mistake," Dorn stated. "A failure. But one failure is nothing. In the end the Great Race—"

"Great Race?" David taunted, backing again as Dorn followed, the other alien close beside him. "How many of your Great Race are there? How long do you think you can go on, hiding, killing, plotting—"

"Enough!" Dorn blared. "There are few of us, and widely scattered, true! But we fight for our lives—and for more than our lives! We fight for a nesting place for our race, that it may yet rise from destruction and live again in the glory it knew a million years ago—!

"Stop!" the second alien barked. "You say too much—" Then he broke into the buzzing speech, his pale eyes fixed on David. Dorn listened, then faced David.

"He is right," he said. "Choose!"

"I've already chosen," David said. "You can go back to the Hell you came from!"

"Kill him," Dorn said simply. "He might have helped us—but in the end it will not matter. He took a step forward. In three months—"!

With a creak and groan, the chandelier shifted, dropped a foot—and caught, jammed. The alien's eyes flashed upward—and as they did, David leaped, caught the rim of the massive assembly, dragged down with all his weight, threw himself aside as, with a rending of wood, the heavy frame came crashing down, squarely across the shoulders of Dorn and his fellow Invader, smashing both of them to their knees.

As David came to his feet, Dorn rose up, lifting the great mass of metal and glass as easily as if it had been made of paper. The second alien, entangled in the dangling pendants, snarled, ripped away a handful of welded ironwork as if it were half-cooked spaghetti.

And at that moment, with a crash like thunder, blue lightning flashed around the rim of the fallen chandelier, crackled in luminous haloes about the ghastly faces of the aliens. The metal glowed red as shock after shock smashed through the metal, through the flesh and bones of the trapped beings, scorching the floor under their feet, lighting the dim room with brilliant arcs of white and blue and yellow. Now the glass was melting, flowing down, spattering in bright droplets. Dorn emitted a tortured shriek, tore at the confining bands, howled anew as the current flickered above his head, smouldered under his coat, bursting into flames. Again, the alien shrieked, and with a final surge, lifted the sparking, crackling mass of sagging, white-hot metal, hurled it from him—

The second alien, rising from the charred floor, emitted a piercing yelp as the spitting, arcing mass slammed against him, pinned him on his back, infolding him in a corruscating corona of blue fire. Dorn whirled, staggered away, struck the wall, smashed half through it; trapped, he hung there, knocking great pieces from the ruined partition in his struggle.

"Vincent. . .did it. . .work?" Thrall's faint voice crackled. "Are you all right. . . ?"

David stumbled to the bookcase where the microphone was hidden.

"Thrall—it worked. You've got to get out now, fast! The house is on fire!"

"I. . .can't move. My legs. . . Too late. Save yourself. . . ."

"I'll come for you!" David dashed for the door, jumped Dorn's hideously branded body, sprinted for the stairs. . .

"Vincent—go back!" Thrall's voice sounded from the wall. "I mustn't. . .let them escape. . .I mean to

. . .blast the house. . .I have explosives placed. . . ready. . ."

"Thrall! Wait!"

"Thirty seconds," Thrall's voice was a weak gasp. "No longer. . .run. . .Vincent. . .I must die. . .But you. . .must live. . .to carry on. . .the fight. . . ."

David halted, looked up the black stairwell. Thrall was up there, alone, crippled. And he would do what he threatened; of that David was certain. There was no time left. And Thrall was right. He himself must not die; he had to live, to fight, and one day win. . .

He whirled, leaped back down, across the great hall, out past the crumbling columns, along the weed-grown drive. . .

". . .twenty-eight. . .twenty-nine. . ." he counted, then dived, rolled behind the shelter of a great oak.

A giant clapped his hands. White light outlined the trees and ragged shrubs in stark brilliance. Under David, the ground trembled, leaped up. A shuddering boom roared out, echoed, echoed, as bits of wood, metal, shattered limbs, a fragment of a polished railing clattered down around him. Rising, David looked toward the house—or toward the spot where the house had been. Now only a smoking pit yawned among out-tilted trees, surrounded by a ring of raw earth, stripped of turf by the mighty blast, scattered with burning timbers.

In the distance, a siren started up, a mournful wail. In a minute or two, there would be people here— police, firemen, curious townsfolk. People who would stand and gape at the ruin that was all that remained of Thrall House. They would cluck and shake their heads—and behind their hands snicker knowingly at this final catastrophe which had overwhelmed their pathetic townsmen.

"They'll remember you as the crazy man who blew

himself up with his insane experiments, Thrall," David said softly. "They'll never know that you died to save them—and millions more—from something they don't even believe in. But I know. Thanks, Thrall. You were a bigger man than any of them. . . ."

Silently, David Vincent moved off across the dark, weed-choked lawn. Half an hour later, from a wooded ridge above the town, he watched as the last of the flames were extinguished—the flames that had wiped out Thrall and with him the aliens.

*"Three months,* Dorn had said. *In three months— what?* There had been certainty in the alien's voice as he had started to blurt his secret—a certainty which boded no good for the planet Earth. Now the chance was gone to learn what he might have said.

But there were others of his kind still alive, still working. *Three months.* What was the plot which would come to fruition then? And what could one man do to stop it?

He didn't know. But he could search on, observe, listen, wait—and perhaps, with luck, before it was too late, he could find the key to the deadly mystery.

David Vincent turned away along the dark path through the woods, silent and alone, to resume the battle against the enemy.

## PART THREE — *THE COUNTERATTACK*

### CHAPTER ONE

A COLD AUTUMN WIND swept along the street, whirling dry leaves into David Vincent's face. He turned up the collar of his coat, plodded on, head down, his legs numb from the hours of walking. . .tramping on and on, with no destination, no end in sight.

He had no idea what time it was, what part of the small midwestern town he was in. It was a faded residential street where small, carelessly maintained houses crouched in ragged yards; houses where children had romped and shouted once, long ago; but now they were silent, dim-windowed, cheerless—caves where the old had crept to die.

David pushed the morbid thoughts from his mind. Vague hunger pangs reminded him that he had not eaten in. . .how long? He didn't remember. He had lost the habit of regular meals these last months, and of regular sleep, regular hours. Day had become a time to wait behind drawn blinds, dozing upright in a chair, listening for the footstep that would mean that they had found him—

Again he thrust the thought away angrily. It was the other way around, he reminded himself. But sometimes, as now, late at night, wandering aimlessly along some strange, cold street, it was hard to remember who was the hunter and who the hunted. The waiting was the worst—waiting for the next move of the enemy. If only there were some way for him to take the iniative, strike at them by surprise. But it was a vain hope. His only course was to go on, watching—and waiting.

A light gleamed ahead through the stark limbs of the gnarled trees lining the cracked sidewalk. He passed the end of a high hedge, saw lighted windows in a tidy brick front set well back from the street. Above the white painted door were the words CEN-TERTON PUBLIC LIBRARY. It looked like an island of warmth and coziness against the backdrop of the indifferent night. On impulse, David turned, went up the brick path.

Inside, an elderly woman in styleless black eyed him over rimless spectacles, taking in his weather-burned face, his chapped knuckles, the battered trench-coat, which hung loose now on his wide-shouldered frame. Her mouth tightened in its nest of wrinkles.

"Was there something you wanted?" she piped, her tone indicating that the library was not a haven in which hoboes were welcome to warm themselves.

"Why, yes," David favored her with a smile. "I'm just in from a field trip; two weeks in the hill country, doing a whooping crane count. Deadly dull work. Just thought I'd drop in and catch up on the scientific journals while awaiting my plane."

"Oh—you're a naturalist?" Her tone changed instantly. "Goodness, I've always been fascinated by bird-watching myself. The whooping crane, you say. Goodness, I had no idea they were to be found in this part of the country!"

"Quite right, they weren't. Still, it was an exhilarating experience." David glanced toward the long table, the comfortable chairs.

"Wouldn't you like to sit down, Mr. .. or is it professor. . . ?" The librarian gushed, won over by the combination of the scholarly approach coupled with David's lean good looks. "I'll bring you the issues you wanted. Which ones . . . ?"

"Ah. . .the Science Digest will do for a start," David said. "Just to give me the big picture."

He took a seat at the far end of the room, with a silent sigh of relief. Suddenly, his accumulated fatigue washed over him like a wave. The warmth of the room was soothing, comforting. . .

He jerked his head up with a start as the librarian placed the magazine before him.

"Sorry," he said. "Almost dozed off. Not used to all that hiking. . ."

"You poor man," the woman clucked. "Would you like a cup of coffee? And I have some crumpets." She lowered her voice. "It's against the rules to eat in the library, of course, but one does get bored, just sitting— and at this hour, I doubt if Miss Wicket is likely to drop in. . ." She almost winked, David thought.

"Wonderful, Miss, ah," he said. "Nothing like a hearty crumpet to stave off collapse."

Eating the dry cookie and sipping the hot coffee, David opened the magazine, leafed through it, his mind on other, less peaceful matters. *Three months,* Dorn had said, the last words he had blurted out before poor Thrall's Invader-trap had, against all likelihood, smashed down on him. *Three months.* It had been a challenge—and a warning. And now the three months were almost gone. Time was running out. And soon—somewhere—the event would occur that had lent the note of triumph to the alien's words. Somewhere—but where? And what? Again, the utter helplessness of his position made David clench his fists in impotent frustration.

With an effort, he calmed himself, cleared his mind. The Invaders were not supermen, he reminded himself. They had strange powers, true, abilities exceeding those of ordinary men. But, on the other side of the coin, they were few, and working in small, isolated cells, against great odds. And most of them— with the notable exception of the one called Dorn— appeared to be little better than servants, near-moronic carriers-out of orders, incapable of original, imaginative action. As for their great strength, their invulnerability to ordinary weapons, that was mere technology, not biological superiority. Their bodies were constructs, organic machines, nothing more.

But this was all familiar ground, the same conclusions, David had reached in the past, mulling over what little he had learned of the Invaders. So little— and so little time left.

And yet—if he made one more effort, dug into the meagre data, extracted all the information possible— perhaps there was something there he had missed, some clue he was overlooking. . . .

There was a pad and pencil on the table. David pulled them to him, began jotting. . . .

An hour later, he had compiled a list—a pitifully short list—of facts relating to the aliens:

1. They are not natives of Earth; ergo, they came here from another world.

2. They can tolerate great heat. Also, their own body temperatures rise very high under stress. Therefore, it's likely they come from a high temperature planet.

3. There are only a few of them. This suggests that either: (a) They represent some sort of small-scale expedition, possibly on a scientific nature, or: (b) they have suffered some disaster which has reduced their numbers.

4. (b) above seems more likely. Based on Dorn's remarks, it appears they intend to take over the planet for their own use.

David paused, re-reading the last item. What was it he had overheard, in the communications room in the tunnel complex inside the dormant volcano? He closed his eyes, remembered the alien voice coming from the TV screen!

"... *brood racks cannot long endure the null-G condition. Nutrient supplies approach exhaustion; energy flow levels dropping rapidly. Contact must be made within one half revolution...*"

Brood racks. The spawn of the aliens. He pictured the Invaders' vessel, lurking somewhere in space, invisible to Earth's crude radar scanners, its hull loaded, not with adult life-forms, but with embryonic creatures, awaiting the preparation of a secure nest below. Then, a landing, the release of hordes of eggs—grubs—whatever form they took. And then, in days or weeks or months—a plague of aliens, bursting out of their hidden brooding places, to overwhelm the unsuspecting planet—

David wiped his hand across his eyes, forcing himself to relax, willing his pulse to slow its hammering. The picture in his mind was as vivid as reality—but it was just a picture. He had to remember that. In the other direction lay madness.

And yet—it fitted. Three months, Dorn had said. It might have been just such a landing he was referring to: the bringing to earth of the brood-ship, ready to lay its eggs in the living flesh of the planet, like a Tsetse fly, depositing its young in the living body of a cow, to hatch and devour the flesh of the unwitting host.

But even with the present primitive state of the world's radar defenses, it would be impossible for an object as large as even a small ship to enter the atmosphere unseen. The Invaders who were already here might have been dropped in tiny, one-alien pods, and thus escaped detection; but a ship would have to show up on the screens. And in the present state of world tension, any object dropping in from a deep space orbit would be the instant object of attention—and of interceptor missiles. And even if they failed to bring it down, it would be tracked, its landing site pin-pointed, surrounded . . .

It made no sense. Dorn's three months deadline HAD to mean a new landing from space. And such a landing was an impossibility.

Unless, of course, all his speculations were in error, all his guesses—just guesses, wild, random ideas, with no relation to reality.

But there was nothing else for him to go on. For all these months, he had watched, scanned faces, read newspapers, searching for anything, any tiniest hint of the Invaders presence—and found nothing. Unless he made assumptions now, he would have to admit defeat; admit himself helpless. And that, David Vincent said silently, fiercely, he would never do!

Unseeing, he turned the pages of the magazine. A picture caught his eye: a photograph of the night sky, streaked across with bright lines.

METEOR SHOWER EXPECTED read the headline beneath it.

David sat staring at the words for a moment. Then, swiftly, he scanned the article. A group of minor rocky bodies had been detected in orbit twenty million miles from Earth, spiraling inward from a previous position beyond Mars. Calculations showed that at their relatively slow velocity of twenty thousand MPH, their path would intersect Earth's orbit in six weeks—on the twenty-seventh day of November—

And this was the twenty-first. David felt excitement stir within him.

He read on. While the main mass of the meteor would clear the Earth by half a million miles, passing beyond the orbit of the moon and continuing on into the sun, the planet's gravitational field might be expected to divert some of the bodies from their course, causing them to take up new orbits around the planet, and eventually enter the atmosphere, where they would be destroyed by air friction, causing a brilliant display in the night sky. The best viewing, the article concluded, would be in the desert area north of Phoenix, Arizona.

David closed the magazine, his mind racing. Earth's astronomers had picked up the approaching swarm six weeks ago; if the Invaders, as he assumed, had a ship orbiting in space nearby, no doubt they could have detected the bodies much earlier—perhaps six months earlier. . . .

Abruptly, more words spoken by the alien communication monitor flashed into his mind:

*"You must wait. . .until the cloud passes. . . ."*

He stood, his chair scraping loudly in the silent room.

"Ohh—must you be going?" the librarian chirped from behind her desk.

"Yes," David said. He buttoned his coat, moving toward the door. "There's not much time left. . ."

"Your plane is leaving now? It's miles to the airport. Shall I call you a cab?"

He looked at the little old lady. Lonely, insecure, with nothing ahead but a few more brief years of thankless puttering among her books—and then the eternal darkness. And yet how bravely she faced the prospect, even gave of her warmth and her small comforts to a passing stranger. David reached out, took her withered hand.

"Thanks," he said. "For being so human. And don't worry. Everything is going to be all right."

The image of her answering smile hung in his mind as he pushed out into the cold wind, leaving the brightness and warmth behind.

## CHAPTER TWO

IT HAD BEEN an all-night bus ride to Springfield, the site of the State University. Now, in mid-morning, bleary-eyed from lack of sleep, David went along the wide, antiseptic corridor of the Bowser Memorial Science Building, reading the neat black lettering on the glass doors. A shapely co-ed emerged from a room ahead, glanced at the tall, gaunt-faced stranger.

"Can. . .can I help you?" she asked hesitantly. She had immense eyes, soft brown hair to her shoulders, a rounded bosom under the bale blue Angora sweater. She looked neat, clean, innocent—a world removed from the fantastic threat of the Invaders.

"I'm looking for Professor Skinner's office," he said. His throat was husky, his voice rough in his own ears.

"Right down that way—at the end of the hall, and to the right." The girl hesitated. "Would you like me to show you?" She moved closer, and David caught a faint odor of a light perfume, of soap, of cleanliness, which made him more aware than ever of his un-shaven face, his rumpled clothes.

"No thanks," he said brusquely. "I can find it on my own."

She nodded almost regretfully, watched him as he went on past her.

Skinner's door was set in an alcove off the main passage. David knocked, and a dry voice called "Come in, come in."

A thin, long-necked man with long wispy white hair and a small, neat goatee looked David over as he entered the narrow, book-cluttered room with a window at the far end affording a view across the campus. He waved a cigaret holder toward a chair.

"Sit down, sit down. Not a student, are you? No, not a student. Not the type." He puffed at the cigaret, blew out smoke, watching David swing the chair around and seat himself. There was a cheerful twinkle in his eyes.

"No, I'm not a student, Professor Skinner. But I was once—about eight years ago."

Skinner looked sharply at him, cocked his head sideways. "Not a science major," he said decisively.

"Engineering," David said.

The professor snapped his fingers, his gold cuff-link catching the light. "Vincent," he said. "Vincent, ah, Solomon?"

"David," he smiled briefly. "David Vincent."

"Of course. I never forget a face. Though yours has changed, I must say. You've seen something of life since I last saw you. I seem to recall—weren't you in Viet Nam. . . ? Something about a decoration?"

David nodded. "Professor, you've read of the meteor swarm that's about to strike Earth?"

Skinner looked surprised at the abrupt change of subject, then adjusted his expression to one of professorial wisdom. "A contradiction in terms, Mr. Vincent," he said complacently. "A meteor, by definition, is a body which does not strike the planetary surface—"

"Yes, Professor, I realize that. But it's my understanding that some of the objects might be drawn into Earth orbit."

"True enough. However, they will burn up in the atmosphere. There's no danger, no danger whatever." He smiled comfortingly.

"Has that been definitely established?" David asked.

Skinner wagged a finger. "You must realize, Mr. Vincent, that most of these bodies are no larger than the head of a pin. Even the most vivid meteorite which you might see streaking across the sky is probably smaller than a pea—and from sixty to two hundred miles above the surface—"

"Yes—but there *are* exceptions."

"True," The professor nodded. "The Johannesburg meteorite, for example, weighed many tons— and of course, Meteor Crater, Arizona—"

"Are the astronomers able to resolve this cloud, determine the size of the individual fragments?"

"Umm. Spectroscopic analysis, plus diffraction techniques are able, to some extent, to determine average particle size. However, as regards meteors of Cometary origin—"

"Cometary origin?"

"Yes. Most of such showers represent the remnants of former comets. The Andromedes, for example—the group about which you're concerned—are the fragments of Biela's Comet, first observed in 1772. Its periodicity was established in 1826, when it was found to follow a typical elliptical orbit, with a period of six years." Skinner waved his cigaret dramatically. "In the passage of 1832, the comet passed very close to Earth. In 1845—it was seen to break in two! By 1852, the two fragments were very faint, and had separated to over a million miles apart. Thereafter, meteor showers were observed annually in its old path. In 1885, for example, almost 40,000 meteors were observed in the space of a few hours, all radiating from the direction of Andromeda—hence the name." The professor leaned back, as if awaiting a show of hands.

"You were saying—about the particle size," David steered the conversation—or lecture—back to the point.

"Oh, yes. As I said, the particles are typically of very small size. The leonids, for example, which were visible earlier this month—"

"I mean specifically in this instance," David persisted. "Has any attempt been made to check on the size of the objects that might fall on Earth?"

"Hardly necessary, Mr. Vincent," Skinner said blandly. "Meteor swarms have been observed since ancient times, and the facts regarding them are well known. The Chaldeans, in 2700 BC, recorded the Perseid shower, for example—"

"Suppose there were larger bodies included in the swarm," David bored on. "Would that fact be apparent from Earth?"

Skinner frowned. "Since the true nature of the swarms has long been known to science, there is no reason to schedule valuable observatory time for the observation of the commonplace, Mr. Vincent," he said. "Are you aware that the use of the major instruments, such as the two hundred inch reflector at Palomar, is scheduled for years ahead?"

"Then it might be possible that a large body *is* on its way to Earth."

"No! Or. . ." Skinner's scientific conscience gave him pause. "I suppose in some theoretical sense it's not a complete impossibility—though I assure you your fears are groundless, Mr. Vincent! Even should a large fragment—even several feet in diameter—strike the earth, it's highly unlikely that it will impact at the precise point you happen to be occupying!"

"It wasn't my personal safety I was concerned about, Professor," David said quietly. "Suppose a multi-ton rock—like the one Peary brought back from the Arctic, for example—impacted in a densely populated area?"

Skinner looked startled. He blinked. "Well—in that case. . .naturally it would be. . ." his voice trailed off; he looked faintly embarrassed. "I'm sorry if I implied that, er. . ."

"That's all right. I just want to confirm that, insofar as we know, it's possible that the swarm includes objects larger than pin-head size."

"Yes, but. . .yes," Skinner nodded, looking thoughtful. "As a matter of fact, Mr. Vincent, it might just be worth having a word with Dr. Shrimpwell. . ." He reached for the phone, dialled a three digit code, murmured a few words into the instrument.

"He can spare us a few moments now," the Professor said, standing. "Let's just pop around to the observatory and lay your fears at rest."

2

"An interesting question, gentlemen," Dr. Shrimpwell said expansively, patting his small, round, Santa Claus tummy. "Of course, our small twelve-inch refractor, here at the University, would be quite incapable of resolving anything smaller than the state of Rhode Island at a distance of two and a half million miles—but the matter might interest a colleague of mine at Mt. Wilson. I'll ring him up, and possibly tonight he can take a look."

David accepted Skinner's invitation to lunch at a

campus restaurant. Over small steaks and French fries, the professor eyed him speculatively.

"Tell me, Mr. Vincent—just what was it that aroused your interest in what, after all, is a purely academic matter? The possiblity, as Dr. Shrimpwell pointed out, of any sizable object being found is of the order of one in several billions."

"Rare enough that if it did show up, it would arouse a certain amount of interest?"

Skinner sighed. "I see you're determined to resist my efforts to pry. As to the interest it might arouse: I'll be candid with you, Mr. Vincent. The public has always demonstrated a profound apathy where abstruse scientific matters are concerned."

"If a large object *is* spotted, what action will be taken?" David persisted.

"Why—none, officially, I suppose. As Dr. Shrimpwell pointed out, the center of the calculated target area is in the western desert. Perhaps a small party mighty be despatched to record the descent, and possibly search for any fragments which might survive the fall. Usually, of course, particles too large to burn entirely away in the initial seconds explode, due to temperature differential."

"Who would send such a party?"

"Interested Universities, perhaps. Private research foundations. The observatories. Even newspapers, in need of Sunday Supplement material—"

"What about the Air Force? The Army?"

Skinner gaped at David. "Whatever for?" His expression changed, became wary. "Mr. Vincent—are you suggesting . . . ?"

"I'm suggesting nothing, Professor," David said flatly. "I'm asking. Just asking."

3

"Remarkable, Mr. Vincent," Dr. Shrimpwell said, his expression less jovial now. "I contacted Dr. Ri—my colleague. He advised me that the presence of a solid body exceeding ten meters in diameter had already been detected in the Andromedes Swarm. The discovery had been kept in strict secrecy since Wednesday last, for fear that premature disclosure might alarm the public. May I ask how you knew of this—and what action you intend to take now? Are you a journalist? I must caution you, misrepresentation—"

"I misrepresented nothing," David cut in. "What do they plan to do about this?"

"Do? Do?" The astronomer puffed out his cheeks, looked indignant. "I presume they will do what the natives of Germany are reputed to do when it rains, sir! Let it rain!"

"Will Mt. Wilson send a crew to observe the fall?"

"The fall? The fall? What fall? There will be no fall, Mr. Vincent—not in the sense I'm sure you mean—a surface strike. There will be no sensational story for your credulous readers, no rabble-rousing article predicting the doom of mankind! I shall, if necessary, lodge a protest with your editor at once! The full weight of this institution will be brought to bear—"

"Calm down, Dr. Shrimpwell," David cut in. "I'm not a reporter."

"He, ah, spoke of the army, Newton," Skinner murmured to his stout colleague. He seems to, ah, fear some, er, hostile, ah, intent. . ."

"Hostile intent?" Shrimpwell drew himself up, compressed his chins menacingly.

"Sir, if it is your intent to involve this University in some insane Invasion From Mars scare, I warn you—"

"Don't warn me, Doctor," David said wearily. "I've been warned by experts."

Outside, Skinner confronted David. "Look here, Vincent—I trust you'll not do anything to further outrage Shrimpwell. . ."

"I won't, Professor." David looked at the agitated pedagogue. "It's strange that you're more worried about the publicity than you are about the object that's about to strike the planet."

"A rock will fall in the desert, nothing more—"

"Are you sure? Absolutely sure?"

Skinner opened his mouth to answer, then closed it again. "I can't help you, Mr. Vincent," he said in a small voice. "But still—well—since you feel as you do, why not refer the matter to the military authorities? Fort Knapp is only a few miles from here. But please: don't—"

"I know," David said. "Don't mention your name."

## CHAPTER THREE

DAVID VINCENT SPENT the whole of the next day at Ft. Knapp, waiting first in one office, then in another. Cold, late-afternoon shadows were lengthening across the floor when he laid aside the dog-eared magazine he had been thumbing for an hour, went to the glassed in office and rapped. The elderly, hard-bitten warrant officer inside slid back the panel.

"Just between the two of us," David said, "Is there any point in my waiting?"

"Just between the two of us—no," the man answered. "Look, fella—we get half a dozen nut cases a week, you know? The colonel hasn't got time—"

"This could be important," David said. "Is there any provision in the regulations for that?"

The man shook his head, smiling crookedly. "Some day maybe we'll miss World War Three on account of the colonel wouldn't see some guy," he said. "In the meantime, this way is easier all around. And by the way," he added as David turned away. "Don't go writing your Congressman you got the cold shoulder or something. Nobody said you couldn't see the man. It's just you got to wait your turn. And you got tired of waiting."

"Right again, Mister." David said wearily.

"Why not give the Air Force a try?" the warrant called after David. "They got a office for what they call Aerial Phenomena over at Carstairs, a couple hundred miles north. Maybe they ain't got such a backlog as we have."

"Thanks for the tip," David said. "I'll try it."

2

The officer seated behind the grey Air Force desk looked at David Vincent with a total absence of expression. His eyes flicked over David's weather beaten trench coat, his scuffed shoes, back to his face, deeply tanned by the open road, a face that reflected the months of strain, of tension, of constant threat.

"Yes, I've seen the reports of the expected meteor shower," the major said in a non-committal tone. "As

Public Information Officer, it's my job to keep abreast of the news. That hardly explains your insistence on seeing me, instead of talking to one of my airmen. They're competent to deal with any, ah, matter you may have to report."

"Did you know that an object at least thirty feet in diameter will probably impact the Earth less than two hundred miles from where we're sitting?" David put the question flatly.

"The major's eyes narrowed. "Where did you learn of this, Mr. Vincent?"

"At *least* thirty feet," David said, ignoring the question. "It might be larger. I'd like to know what the Air Force is doing about it?"

"Doing? What do you expect us to do, Mr. Vincent? Meteorites are outside Air Force jurisdiction, I'm afraid." He smiled sourly.

"These are troubled times, Major, David said. A large object is headed toward the planet—toward the United States, to be specific. It's due to arrive in less than eighteen hours. I wonder if it occurred to you that it might be advisable to keep it under close scrutiny as it comes in—and have a force standing by on the spot when it hits."

"What the devil are you implying?" the major snapped. "That this is cover for a Communist attack?"

"I didn't say anything about Communists. In fact, it might be wise to call the Russians in on this, to get complete coverage while the object is out of sight from our side of the planet."

"Call in the Russians, eh? What are you, Mr. Vincent—some kind of home-grown Red?"

"Forget politics," David said. "I'm talking about a possible threat to the planet."

"A threat to the planet?" the major echoed incredulously.

"A meteor swarm might be a good place to hide a weapon, Major," David said levelly.

The officer's face flushed. "My time is valuable," he said curtly. "I have half a dozen reports to complete today, four inspections to make, a staff meeting—"

"This is more important than a staff meeting, Major," David said flatly.

"Are you suggesting that it's all a diabolical plot by the little green Martians?" the major barked. "If so, I suggest you see a psychiatrist! You'll find the Invaders exist only in your own tortured imagination!"

"Invaders?" David said softly. "Who said anything about Invaders?"

"It's the classic pattern: delusions of persecution, imaginary enemies, monsters from outer space!" The major rose, faced David, his face set in lines of fury. "Why is it you world-savers always imagine you're unique?" he grated. "You picture yourselves rushing in to do what all the trained men and equipment of an organization have missed! Don't you know I see hundreds like you in the course of a year—publicity hungry, neurotic shadow-jumpers—the saucer sighters, the spy-suspecters, the hidden bomb alarmists, here to tip the Air Force off to the end of the world? Well, Mr. Vincent, I've got better things to do with my time than listen to another announcement of doom! I have work to do! Work that won't wait! It may not be as exciting as a story about silver lizard men coming up through the sewers, but at least it makes sense! Good day, Mr. Vincent! The sergeant will show you out!" The furious officer pressed a buzzer on his desk, sank back in his chair, breathing hard.

"Thanks," David said as the door opened and a stocky, thick-shouldered man in stiff khakis stepped through. "You confirmed my first impression: I'm wasting my time here."

"See that this man leaves the base—at once!" the major snapped. His eyes were still glaring at David's back as the door closed behind him.

### 3

David followed the impassive non-com along the grey-painted corridor, past the open doors of offices where typewriters clacked in workaday fashion, through a walnut-paneled foyer decorated with posters plugging the latest economy drive, out into the hot, white mid-day sunlight.

"Thanks, Sergeant," he said. "I'll go quietly; or does the major expect you to hold my hand all the way to the gate?"

The grizzled NCO spat in the flower bed, shot David a sharp look.

"I heard some of what you said," he rumbled in a deep baritone voice. "About the meteor shower. I read about that. Supposed to hit north of here, right?"

"That's right."

"Nothing so unusual about that," the sergeant went on, as if talking to himself. "Meteors hit the atmosphere all the time, couple thousand a day all over the world. . ."

"This time it's a little different," David said. "There's a big one in among the gravel."

"And?" the NCO eyed David curiously.

"And I'm curious."

The NCO nodded, indicated a staff car parked before the headquarters building. Silently, he took the wheel, drove along the neat, militarily precise street.

Off to the left, behind a high fence, David saw massive dun-colored vehicles parked in rows: light and medium tanks, half-trucks, recon cars. They looked dusty, abandoned.

"Belong to the Army," the sergeant said, noting the direction of David's glance. "Emergency stuff, mothballed. And if I know the brass, they'll stay that way."

As David got out of the car at the gate, the sergeant leaned across to speak to him.

"I saw something once, Mr. Vincent—something I never told anybody about. If you're interested—I usually have a drink, about seven PM, at a little place called Gunner's Grill, in town, on Adams Street." Without waiting for an answer, he wheeled the blue-painted sedan in a U turn and drove away.

4

It was a small, quiet bar, dim-lit, sparsely patronized at this hour. David took a booth at the rear, ordered a Scotch and water. He had taken no more than a sip of the drink when a bulky figure slid into the seat across from him.

"You look different in civilian clothes," David said. "What will you have?"

"Beer. Yeah, everybody thinks a guy was born in that blue suit, once they see him in it. But underneath it, I'm just another civilian, Mr. Vincent." The man nodded as the waiter put glasses on the table and went away. "Enough of a civilian to wonder about some of the things that go on at the base," he added.

"You overheard the major's brush-off?"

"They've got it all on tape," the sergeant said. "They know all the answers. And the answers they don't know they don't want to hear about. . . ." He took a pull at the beer, looking at nothing.

"That's why you didn't tell anyone about whatever it was you saw," David prompted.

"Yeah. I'd of been psyched out on my ear." The sergeant looked directly at David. "Look mister—I'm putting my stripes in your hands, talking to you. But from where I sit, I hear lots of things. That door's not too thick. I don't say much, but I listen good. Those people aren't all nuts, Mr. Vincent. Lights in the sky, yeah, maybe it's the planet Venus, or a weather balloon, or just a B-55 from the base. But when a guy sees something like I saw. . ." He paused, took another deep draft from his glass. "Either there's something going on, or I'm as crazy as they'd call me if I turned it in."

"Just exactly what did you see, Sergeant?"

The NCO took a deep breath. "It was just about a year ago," he said. "I was on leave, visiting my sister in St. Louis. We took a drive one evening—just roaming around the countryside, talking about how we used to hike around there when we were kids. We parked the car, and climbed up to where there were some big trees—a place we used to come for picnics, you know. She had a basket of sandwich makings along. While she was setting up for lunch, I took a hike up to the top. Nice view up there. I was just about to start back down, when I noticed something kind of funny. I mean, it was a place where nobody else much used to come—but here were these tire tracks, it looked like—a pair of parallel grooves in the dirt. I looked closer, and saw they ran right across the ground, across rock—cut right through it, like it was soft as cheese. Ran on off into deep brush. I followed 'em." The sergeant paused to finish his glass, signalled for another.

"They ran into the brush, like I said," he continued. "And about twenty feet back from the edge of the clearing, I found the thing that made 'em. It was about the size of an old fashioned baby carriage—you know, the kind with the wicker top that came up. It was lying on its side, and there were a pair of runners, bent up pretty bad; that was what made the marks. It was open—and empty. I went up close, looked inside. There was nothing there but what looked like a bunch of spun glass. But there was a hollow in the stuff, like an Easter basket with the eggs gone."

The waiter brought the fresh drinks. The sergeant looked at the table-top, waiting for the man to finish.

"I turned around then, to start back, and I saw—it." His teeth went together in a silent snarl. "Like a pile of dirty, orange-colored rot, it was. A filthy looking mess, foamy, like some kind of slimy fungus. And in the middle of it—something was moving. I stopped dead, and watched it. How can I describe it? A fifty pound oyster, without a shell. A lump of grey meat, meat that squirmed. I tell you, Mr. Vincent, I was sick! I looked around for a stick, anything; if I'd had a gun, I'd have blasted it! I can feel my skin crawling now, thinking about it..." the man broke off, shuddered. His tough, sun-tanned face was greenish pale.

"What did you do then?" David asked quietly.

I found my stick—a good sized club, six feet long. I started toward the mess—and it buzzed at me." The airman's eyes were on David's face, sick eyes, filled with horror. "That buzz—like a rattler's warning. It went right between my bones. I dropped the stick and backed away. Then I noticed something else. All around the thing, the ground was bare. The bushes were dead, brown, dried out. I wanted to yell, but all that came out was a kind of a croak. And a smell was coming from it—a smell like iodine. And then—then it started toward me. . ." The man gulped half his beer, shuddered. "I ran, Mr. Vincent. I ran all the way back to where my sister was, with the lunch all ready, and I yelled at her to come on, and I grabbed her arm, and dragged her all the way back to the car. Left the lunch basket, everything. She thought I was crazy, out of my mind—but I couldn't tell her what I'd seen. I drove into town as fast as I could go, meant to report the thing to the police, the state cops, anybody—but by the time I got there, I changed my mind." He looked at David defiantly. "My own sister thought I was crazy, just for running from it. I started thinking about what the cops would say. And when word got back to my outfit ..." the non-com smiled lop-sidedly. "The major's got no use for crackpots, Mr. Vincent. In his job, he sees too many of 'em."

"So you just let it go at that?"

The NCO shook his head. "By the next day I was beginning to think I'd gone off half-cocked; that if there was really anything there, it couldn't have been as bad as what I thought. After all, a pile of fungus—or even a dead body—that was what I was starting to think by then—a decayed corpse—wasn't all that bad. I was supposed to be a military man; Hell, I've seen combat, I know what it's like to hear flak whistling past my ears. This wasn't like that.

"But I took a camera and went back up, alone, the next day. I found the place, all right—but. . .*it* was gone."

"No trace of it left?" David asked.

"There was a little brownish crust where it had been—and the dead bushes, just like I remembered, and the nest. But the worst part. . . ."

"The worst part, Sergeant?"

"From the spot where I saw the thing, there was a trail. It led across the clearing, down the slope. I lost it on the rocks."

"What kind of trail?"

"Footprints." The non-com's voice was hoarse with strain.

"You mean—animal tracks?"

"No, Mr. Vincent. Not animal prints. They were human. Bare, human footprints. They came from the nest. Whatever it was I saw grew feet, Mr. Vincent—and got up and walked away!"

5

"A thing like that," the sergeant said. "out there in the middle of nowhere. Where did it come from—and where did it go? That's what scares me, Mr. Vincent. Where did it go?"

"Listen to me, Sergeant," David said urgently. Across from him, the man's face was slack, his cheek twitching; he reached for his beer glass, spilled part of it getting it to his mouth.

"Listen to you? What for? You can't tell me. You can't answer the question that's been eating my mind out for a year now. I know what I saw! I know!"

"All right, you know," David caught the man's wrist. "What do you plan to do about it, cry in your beer?" His voice cracked like a whip.

"Wha—what else can I do? Nobody'd believe me—"

"I believe you."

"Yeah?" the man's eyes were bleary now, haggard. "Who're you? Just a civilian. You can't help. Nobody can help. I'm going crazy." He gripped his head, rocked back and forth. "I'm going out of my mind, and nobody can help me—"

"You can help yourself—unless you're willing to curl up and die without a fight," David said harshly.

"Fight? I'll fight! But who'm I going to fight? And what? What kind of man is it that's born in a garbage pile in the woods, all by himself? What—"

"Shut up a minute," David said in a steady tone, "And I'll tell you."

The man looked at him. "You?" It was almost a plea. "You think you know what it was? That I'm not losing my mind?"

"What you saw was an alien, Sergeant. A lone creature, dropped here in a sort of larval form, to mature quickly and then set out to do what it was sent here to do. It was just one of many. I've seen a few of them. They look like men, but they're not men. And their plans are simple: to take over the earth."

The airman goggled at David. "Geeze!" he muttered "A guy nuttier than I am!"

"Maybe," David smiled grimly. "But you saw the thing—I didn't."

"Yeah—that's right. I saw it. God help me, I saw it—and I wish I never had!"

"But you did. And now you know what it was you saw—and why it's here. Now—are you willing to help me fight it?"

"How? We don't even know where they are, what they're doing!"

"Remember the meteorite?" David said.

"You mean—you think there's some connection. . . ?"

"Maybe."

The man nodded slowly, his eyes on David's. "So?"

"So I want to be there waiting when the big one hits. I've tried to interest people in it, Sergeant. I got nowhere. Now time's running out. I'm afraid it's up to you and me."

"What have you got in mind? What can a couple of guys do. . . ?"

"You remember those armored vehicles parked at the base?"

"Sure. What about 'em?"

"You can help me steal one."

"Steal a tank from the Army? Now I know you're off your rocker!"

"Could it be done?"

The sergeant opened his mouth, closed it again. He nodded. "Maybe; yeah, it could be done. I know a couple angles. But—"

"Good," David said, rising. "Let's get started. We haven't got much time."

## CHAPTER FOUR

HALF AN HOUR after sunset, Sergeant Joseph Anoti braked his battered station wagon to a halt at the side of the dirt road which ran beside the field of dry cornstalks bordering the Air Base on the north. A quarter of a mile distant, the lights of the flightline hangars glowed through the dusk.

"We could cut the fence anywhere along here to get in," Anoti said. "But the trick is to get back out with the vehicle. That means we use Gate Six, over there to the right. It opens onto the Taxiway. We can make our touch on the north side of the lot—one of the half-tracks, I'd say—and instead of heading for the ramp, swing right, across the end of Runway 020! The gate hasn't been used for maybe ten years; it's pretty well grown up in weeds. But there's the remains of an old blacktop road that cuts across the south end of the field there. If we do it nice, maybe they won't spot us. It's far enough off at the end of the base that—"

"We'll have to take our chances," David cut into the Sergeant's rationalizations. "You take the jerricans; I'll handle the batteries." He stepped from the car, sweating in the Air Force blues lent him by Anoti—a crude disguise in case of emergency. Heavy laden with equipment the two men crossed the cornfield, concealed by the dry, unharvested stalks, victims of a year of less than normal rainfall. They crossed the abandoned blacktop road, scrambled through a weed-choked ditch, reached the fence. Anoti used a pair of heavy issue binoculars to scan the area for patrolling Air Police.

"It's clear," he muttered. "Let's go."

At the gate, a sturdy construction of galvanized pipe and wire mesh, still intact after years of neglect thanks to the dry climate, the sergeant tried keys in the heavy padlock. On the fifth attempt, it opened with a squeal of unoiled metal. He pulled the gate back a foot and they slipped through.

"OK, from here it's gravy," he said. "Until we start up, that is. And if my idea works right—"

"Let's try it and see," David suggested. He led the way in the shadows along the fence; in the shelter of the parked armor, they angled in, a minute later were among the mothballed behemoths, looming dark against the blue-black sky.

Anoti slapped the rust-streaked flank of a half-tracked ammunition carrier, mounting a 50 calibre machine gun atop the armored cab. "What about this baby?" he proposed. "I checked out in one like this, back before there was an Air Force."

"Good enough," David agreed. Working swiftly and silently, the two men hoisted the big twelve volt battery into place under the hood, used the tools they had brought to connect the corroded terminals.

"OK," Anoti said. "She's hot. Dump the gas in and I'll check in back." David poured five gallons in the tank and a cupful in the carburetor.

"OK back here," Anoti called. "Two thousand rounds of armor-piercing, in belts, cases sealed. But don't crank her yet." He took a metal cannister from the tool kit, crawled under the 'track, attached it to the end of the exhaust pipe.

"Home-made muffler," he said. "Use it test-running my dragster so the neighbors don't gripe too much. It ought to cut her down to a low purr."

In the driver's seat, David tried the starter; the big engine, still well-oiled, turned over with a groan, then more easily, it sputtered softly, barked a muffled backfire, caught and ran smoothly.

"She sounds like an old lady's pet Caddie," Anoti said as he swung up beside David. "OK, Vincent, let's get out of here before some of these AP's sneak over this way for a nap and stumble over us."

Almost silently, without lights, the low-slung track moved out, concealed by the ranked vehicles, reached the gate, pulled out on the unused road. Anoti jumped down, closed the gate behind them. "OK," he muttered as he clambered back into his seat. "All clear for points north—and don't spare the horses."

2

"Only two hours left," Anoti said, glancing at the glowing dial of his wristwatch. "And we've still got sixty miles to cover." In the dim dash lights, his heavy features were grim, determined—and at the same time, more relaxed than David had seen him before. "We'll make the next forty easy on the Interstate, then Switch to State 101 for the last stretch." He frowned. "We'll have to leave the road here. . ." he pointed to the folded map in his hand with a blunt forefinger. "I wish we had a better fix on that target area."

"Plus or minus ten miles was the best figure I could get," Davis said. "I had to twist a certain professor's arm pretty hard to get that much. And he made it plain it was just an educated guess, at that. We might be off by fifty miles."

"In that case, we're sunk." Anoti gnawed his lip. "Listen; I know a guy in meteorology, back at the base. Maybe if we stop up the line someplace, I give him a call. . . ."

"Good idea."

An hour later, with new data confirming the original target area, David wheeled the 'track off the expressway, bumped down a pot-holed approachway to a narrow state road. After half an hour, Anoti pointed ahead.

"Up there by the billboard, Vincent. That'll be the county line where the road swings east. I say we should peel off there."

David steered the armored car down across a gravelled shoulder, up a steep bank to level ground. Ahead, a wasteland of rock-strewn desert stretched to a moonlit mountain range on the horizon.

"Rough looking country," Anoti commented. "A good place to disappear in," David said. "They'll have missed the car by now—and we won't be hard to trace."

"Another half hour and it won't matter," Anoti said.

"Unless your meteor shower is late."

"It won't be. And we'd better not be either." David put the heavy car in gear and headed out into the vast desolation.

3

"Look!" Anoti grabbed at David's arm. A faint white arc streaked across the sky. "And there's another one!"

"Those are just a few advance guards," David said, steering on into the dusty lane of light cast by his headlamps. "We're almost to ground zero now; another mile and we'll start looking for a spot to hole up."

More bright streaks appeared, radiating from a point high over the eastern horizon. The ground here was rolling, a series of shallow depressions angling across their path, separated by low ridges. David slowed as the headlight's beam caught a hillock topped by a massive boulder, upraised by some long-past glacier.

"How about that?" he suggested.

"Looks OK to me," Anoti said. "Let's get set, so I can break out that ammo and get ready to say hello."

David pulled the 'track up the steep slant of rock, parked it in the lee of the multi-ton slab of limestone. Anoti used a bar to open cases, lay out the heavy links of finger-thick cartridges.

"A hundred rounds to a belt," he said. "According to the alert plan, this is supposed to be all fresh stuff, less than a year old." He unclamped the barrel of the big water-cooled gun, traversed and elevated it. It moved smoothly, silently.

"She looks good," he said, after checking the receiver mechanism. He fed in the end of a belt, jacked the lever.

"Ready to go," he said. Beside him, David was scanning the sky with the binoculars. The meteorites, like streaks of briefly luminous chalk on a vast blackboard, were flaring thick and fast now, scarcely a second apart. One, brighter than the others, burned its way down in a long curve almost to the horizon, then burst in a spray of silent fire.

"Wow!" Anoti breathed. "Some fireworks!"

"That was no pin-head," David said. "It—"

"Hey!" Anoti hissed. "Listen!"

David turned his head slowly—and heard a soft, stealth scraping. It came from the shadowy jumble of rocks downslope.

"There's somebody down there," Anoti whispered through his bared teeth. He swung the gun silently around, aimed it downslope.

"Hold your fire," David said softly. "But be ready." He slipped over the side, moved away from the car, a dark shadow among shadows. He skirted the scatter of rock fragments, worked his way down almost to the level, then traversed the bottom of the slope. Now looking up, he could see the path clear to the high silhouette of the rock by which the car was hidden. And in that space, something moved: a hunched figure, scuttling awkwardly. David moved quickly up behind a screen of rocks, paralleling the other's course. Emerging from between two slabs, he saw the furtive figure crouched twenty feet from him.

As the figure rose to move foward, David switched on the big ten cell flashlight he carried, directed the beam full in the man's face.

"Hold it right there," he snapped. "Joe!" he called. "If he moves, open up!"

The startled intruder half whirled as the light

struck him; David caught only a glimpse of stark, age-ravaged features before the man whipped up the corner of his tattered sheepherder's cloak to shield his eyes. Under his faded garments, his limbs were crooked, gnarly, his back twisted. He stood unmoving as David came up, stopped ten feet from him.

"Who are you?" David demanded, hearing the harshness in his own tone. "What are you doing out here?" Pale light flashed on the old man's seamed forehead, his colorless garments, flashed again as meteorites burned their way across the sky.

"Hey—what's an old geezer like that doing out here in the middle of noplace?" Anoti called. "Brother, he gave me a scare for a second—"

"Hold that gun on him," David snapped. Again he spoke to the old man. The latter stood in a half-crouch, as though paralyzed with fear. He made no reply.

"Probably a Mexican," Anoti called. "*Ai, babo, che vuoi? . . . Perche non parlano. . . ?*

The old man turned slowly toward the voice from the darkness. Still he made no sound.

Probably he can't talk," Anoti said. "You know, deaf and dumb. But listen, Vincent, never mind this guy! We've got other things to do right now!" Upslope, his bulky shape atop the half-track was visible now in the flickering light as meteors fell by the half dozen, illuminating the landscape like summer lightning. "The poor old bum is probably scared to death," Anoti said. "Superstitious, you know. Leave him be—" He broke off as a vivid light flared above, burning its way across the sky.

"My God, Vincent! Look!"

David stared upward at the swelling brilliance. "That's our baby," he called. "And it looks like we're in the right spot to welcome it!"

## CHAPTER FIVE

As DAVID RACED up the slope, the line of fire length-
ened, arcing over, down, down. Now a rumble like a
distant freight train was audible, increasing steadily
in intensity. "It's going to land right on top of us!"
Anoti yelled. "Let's get out of here!"

"Hold it!" David barked, grabbing the other's arm.
"It just looks like it's headed straight for us! The odds
are it won't hit within a couple of miles at the closest!
This is what we came for, remember?"

"Yeah—but. . ."

"From two hundred miles up, it will take it about a
minute to reach the ground," David called over the
rising thunder. Now the meteor was a blazing fireball,
rushing swiftly closer, dropping, dropping.

"My God, look at it!" Anoti shouted. "You can feel
the heat from here—!"

"That's your imagination," David shouted in his ear.
The light was blindingly bright now, like a new-risen
sun. The fireball's shape changed, elongated. Suddenly it separated into two parts. The smaller portion
moved away from the parent object, which plum-
meted on, plunging straight down—

The blast lit the sky from horizon to horizon. From
the point of impact—perhaps five miles distant—a
graceful fountain of crimson jetted slowly up, glaring
a fiery red as the glow died across the sky, falling
back to a pit of white-hot incandescence.

"My God!" Anoti started—and at that mom

noise struck: wave after wave of deafening sound, like the crashing of a titanic surf. David clapped his hands over his ears, almost fell as the shock wave rocked the car, started small stones bounding down the slope.

"What. . .what. . . ?" Anoti croaked. He had fallen, and blood trickled from a cut on his cheekbone.

"That was it!" David yelled. In his ears, his own voice sounded remote, far away. "That was the ship separating! It had to be! The thing was below the radar horizon for the nearest installation! All the instruments will read is a massive body dropping in, followed by the impact!"

"Yeah—but where did it go?" Anoti was on his feet, staring wildly into the darkness. "Vincent, we're out of our class! That thing was the size of a battleship! And us with a popgun—!"

"Look!" David pointed. Low above the horizon, lights moved, travelling on a course that angled toward their position.

"That's it!" Anoti jumped down, grabbed for the cab door. "Vincent, we've got to get help!"—

"Too late," David snapped. "By the time we got back, it would be all over! We've got to handle it the best we can!"

"It's coming this way!"

"We'll wait until it stops, then make our play."

In silence, the two men watched as the lights moved steadily nearer. Now they could make out the dull gleam of reflected light on a surface that flared out below the horizontal light slits. Half a mile distant, the vessel halted, hung in the air, perhaps twenty feet above the rocky ground, a cold blue glare shining from its underside. Slowly, panels unfolded, reaching downward, settling against the ground.

"Hail Mary, full of grace...." Anoti muttered half aloud.

"All right, let's go!" As David put his hand on the side of the car to jump down, there was a flicker of motion off to the left. Anoti whirled as the old man sprang toward the car.

"Hey!" he yelled. "What the—" He jumped forward, caught at the old man's arm—

There was a blur of motion, and Anoti whirled up, over, to slam stunningly against a boulder. He sprawled, moving feebly.

"Vincent," he croaked as the old man crouched, as if ready to spring. 'The way he moved—like lightning! And he's strong! Watch out, Vincent..."

David had already reached for the grips of the machine gun, swung it to cover the old man, who turned slowly, staring up at him with strange, pale eyes—

Eyes that he had seen before. Ochre eyes, blazing with yellow fire....

The old man straightened, dropped the arm with which he had covered his face, exposing features twisted and knotted with scars, drawn into a grimace of pain and hate. David felt icy cold strike through him as he looked into the ruined face of the unkillable alien, Dorn.

2

"Yes, David Vincent," Dorn's voice was a thin rasp, a shadow of its former vibrant strength. "I still live! Does it shock you to look at what you've done to me?" With a savage gesture, the alien threw back the ragged cloak, tore open the faded shirt beneath it. Sick with horror, David stared at the gnarled, knotted mass of scar tissue that covered the creature from chin to navel.

"You burned my body, broke my bones," Dorn keened. "And now, again, you aim a weapon at me! But I ask you—as one living being to another—hold your fire!"

"Don't move," David said between gritted teeth.

"Vincent. . ." Anoti croaked. "Shoot him—he's not human—can't you see—"

"That's right," Dorn cut in. "Shoot the alien, kill the stranger! That's the way of your tribe, is it not, Vincent? You boast of your civilization, your enlightenment, your mercy! And yet you've hunted me and my kind like vermin! Dorn's eyes seemed to gleam in the fitful glow of the silent, flaring meteorites. "Does not the sight of your handiwork sicken you, David Vincent?"

"I took my cue from you, Dorn!" David's voice was ragged. "You killed four men in my sight; you killed a factory manager named Winthrop, and unless I'm mistaken, you killed General Moore—and God knows how many others. You dumped my friend, Al Lieberman out of your copter to die—"

"Listen to me, Vincent!" Dorn hissed, urgency in his voice. "Consider our plight—and be merciful! We are few—strangers, and afraid, outnumbered a million—ten million to one! Yes, we killed—but out of fear, caution—out of our desperate need to keep our presence secret! It was an error, I see that now! But how could we know? We searched for so long, Vincent, to find a world where we could survive! A million years have passed since our world died—burned to vapor in the explosion of our sun! Only we escaped—one shipload, out of all the billions of the Great Race! For a thousand millennia we've cruised across the void, searching, searching! A thousand of us have lived and died, serving out our lonely hundred years tours of duty, scanning each sun, studying each planet, tending the brood racks where the larva wait for the day when once again we can give them life! And at last—we found this world, Vincent! Almost too late, we found it! We find it cold its sun dim—but still —we can survive here! And survive here we must, or die for all eternity! Our fuel, our supplies are exhausted! We managed to bring our vessel to orbit, far beyond your moon. A few of us—volunteers—have descended to scout out the terrain, find nesting sites. Would you deny us that? Would you be guilty of genocide, the most heinous of all crimes?"

"You haven't given us much choice," David said. "You came as enemies—and mankind has a way of fighting back against attack—"

"I admitted that was an error! Dorn croaked. "But it's not too late to correct it! Now our first brood-vessel lands there, half a mile away. Lay aside your weapon, Vincent! Welcome us in peace! Let us share your world, and in return—"

With a sudden yell, Anoti came to his feet.

"Don't listen to him, Vincent! He's lying!" As he shouted the words, he sprang at the hunched figure— and Dorn whirled with inhuman swiftness, struck out, one devastating blow. David heard the sickening crunch of bone, saw Anoti's crumpled body tumble back like a broken doll into the dust, blood gushing from his mouth, his chest smashed into pulped flesh.

And in the same instant, David's fists tightened on the machine gun's triggers. Sound smashed out, and vivid, stuttering light. Dorn staggered back amid the shriek of ricochets as the steel-jacketed slugs poured into him ripping the clothing from his body. He tottered, regained his balance, stood for a moment, rock-

ing to the shocking impact, staring up at David
Vincent through that terrible fire, his rag flapping as
if in a high wind. Then he advanced, step by step,
directly into the flaming muzzle of the gun. One
step—a second—and he halted, his scarred face
twisted into a mask of impotent fury; then, as though
some inner reservoir of strength had been suddenly
exhausted, he jerked, staggered backward. His head
jerked; one eye exploded from its socket. Pieces flew
from his torso, stripped of its rage. And still the
armor-piercing slugs hosed into that near-indestruct-
ible body, smashing, ripping, tearing—

Slowly, Dorn fell, kicking and flailing. David followed with the stream of tracers, saw the twisted
arms reach, the crooked fingers scrabble, pulling the
severed torso toward him, while the lower body, left
behind, thrashed among the rocks. And as the last
round of the belt smacked into the maimed thing, it
gave a final shudder and fell still, the outreaching
hands only inches from the iron treads of the vehicle.
In the echoing silence that followed, the smashed,
torn face turned upward, the shattered jaw moved.

"More. . .of us. . .will come. . ." the dying voice
whispered. "The Great Race. . .will not die. . . ."

Then it fell silent, and David was alone, under the
nightmare sky.

3

A thousand yards away across the expanse of barren rock, the alien vessel rested in a pool of blue
light. For a long moment, David stared at it, half-
stunned by the violence of the preceding seconds.
Then he jumped down, swung into the drivers seat,
started up the engine, slammed the half-track in gear,
gunned down the slope. A vivid point of light glared

suddenly near the top of the alien craft; a shaft of pale light speared out, smoking across the ground toward him. David wrenched the wheel hard, veered to the right into the shelter of a line of rock slabs, thundered on over rough ground in the darkness. Ahead, a narrow gap appeared on the left. He braked, swung between tank-sized boulders, and slammed to a stop. Dead ahead, less than two hundred yards away, the alien ship shed its ghostly light on the rocky ground. In that light, creatures moved. Not humanoids, these, but monstrous grotesqueries, like some nightmare seathings, hauled up from the eternal darkness of the ocean's abysmal depths. There were six of them, knobbed and spined, moving on rows of stubbed appendages. Seven, eight, David counted; and still more poured from the vessel, working with frantic haste to erect a spidery framework, rigging cables and power lines from the vessel.

*Brooding racks,* Dorn had said. What the term might mean, David didn't know—but in his mind was the image of seething nests of embryonic grubs, planted somewhere—far underground, or broadcast across the landscape in billions, to grow into the fungoid horrors of which Anoti had seen a sample—and to mature with terrifying speed into full-grown Invaders, super-human, unkillable—

David caught himself. *No—not unkillable! Not* quite. Dorn had been tough—but the bullets had ripped *him in two. And there were more belts ready. . . .*

But the range was too great. He had to be sure; there would be no second chance...

Savagely, he gunned the engine, and the powerful armored vehicle charged from its hiding place, roaring down on the alien vessel and its nightmare crew. For a moment, through the dust-streaked windshield,

David saw no indication that they were aware of his precipitous approach; then two of the creatures nearest the access ladder whirled, their multiple limbs rippling, flowed back up inside the hull. A moment later, the searchlight beam winked on, raked across the ground toward him. Instinctively, David cut the wheel, veering from the path of the pale, ominous light—but it reversed, swept back, blazed full in his face—dazzling, scorching hot!

David ducked down behind the dash, saw the paint bubble and smoke on the metal above him, saw the steering wheel sag and flow, saw smoke pour from the upholstered seat back. The windshield blew inward, scattering globs of molten glass which scorched his jacket, blistering where they touched his skin. Flames leaped up, whipped by the wind shrieking through the empty windshield frame. Still holding the gas pedal to the floor, David fought to hold the wheel steady, in spite of the searing pain in his hands.

A terrific shock rocked the speeding car, ripping the wheel tore from David's grasp. Helplessly, he felt the heavy machine careen to the left in a wild skid, felt it tilting, saw the searching heat-beam flash on the upwhirled cloud of dust—

Then a world-ending smash, a sense of falling, a tumult of sound, of light, that faded, faded, into endless blackness. . . .

4

Buzzings, like the angry buzzings of bees, when their hive is disturbed. Harsh lights that flickered, died, flickered, cutting through the soft cocoon of darkness, bringing him back to consciousness, to awareness, to—

A terrible pain shot through David's head. He

groaned, reached up, felt a deep gash across his scalp. The side of his face was covered with blood, the front of his borrowed Air Force blouse sodden. He tried to move, found his legs pinioned by weight across them. He groped, found a grip, with an effort that wrenched a groan from his lips, pulled himself sideways. The half-charred seat toppled off him at the movement. The car was on its side; his shoulder was wedged against sand that filled the smashed window opening. Painfully, he dragged himself upright, wiped blood from his eye, looked out at a scene like a Medieval conception of Hell.

Against the backdrop of the meteor-streaked sky, the alien machine bulked pearly grey, as big as a barn, less than a hundred feet from him. Long shadows moved in the blue glare—shadows of fantastic shape. From this distance, David could see the scaled, grey skin, the networks of purple blood vessels across the pale undersides, the stiff bristles studding the short limbs—and the straps and pouches buckled around those hideous bodies, that told more plainly than words that these monstrous things were motivated by an intelligence that equalled or exceeded that of man.

He heard another buzz, close at hand; something slithered down across the side of the car, dropped to the ground with a heavy thump. David froze, his eyes slitted, as a dark shadow loomed for a moment beside him. Pale, piercing yellow eyes gazed in at him. He didn't breathe, didn't move. . . .

The eyes moved on; the creature turned away. David watched it ripple back to rejoin its fellows. Apparently he had been left for dead. Slowly, with infinite care, David pushed up, past the melted steering wheel, reached the opposite window, empty of glass. There was no alarm as he thrust his head out.

The aliens, contemptuous of man, having seen him lying in the wreck, blood soaked, were taking no further interest in him—he hoped.

He pulled himself up through the opening, slid down across the dented roof to the ground. The machine gun rested at a crooked angle, half-ripped from its mounting, its muzzle pointing down at the rocks. Quickly, David ran his hands over it. As far as he could tell, it seemed to be intact. He gripped it, swung the barrel up, up, wedged it against the edge of the roof. Working in the deep shadow of the car, he straightened out the twisted belt of ammunition. As he did, the end slipped, clattered loudly against the car. At once, one of the alien beings snapped erect, spun, headed toward his position.

"OK, you'll do to start with," David muttered—and squeezed the paired triggers.

Fire boomed and smashed as the powerful gun roared out its message of destruction. The advancing alien halted, gave a convulsive shake and went down. David saw dark fluid well from a dozen gaping wounds in its underside. He traversed the gun, swiftly, caught a second alien as it charged toward him and another pair as they labored to drag a heavy beam upright. They fell, and the beam with them, bringing down another section of the construction. Two more of the creatures leaped in to save the structure, bucked and writhed under the hail of bullets, went down, flopping and humping in the sand. But there were more—too many more. As David swept the nearest of them with his withering fire, others raced for the shelter of the vessel, disappeared up the short access ramp. David raised his sights, poured fire against the hull—but in vain. The high velocity slugs failed to mark the strange material. And then the heat-beam winked on, cut around sharply to bear on the car. A tire burst into flame; the metal of the gun's shield glowed cherry red, then white. David held on, firing at the open entry, until the metal scorched his hands. . . still he hung on; pouring in the fire. . . . At last he stumbled back, the insistent whine of the energy ray all about him. He saw the beam eat through the car's armored side, laying bare the frame, the fuel tank—

David turned to run, felt his legs collapse under him. He went down, slamming his face against rock. Half-dazed, he crawled, heading for the shelter of an outcropping of rock—

Light fountained behind him; metal whined past his head, clanged off rock. He saw one of the half-track's wheels, its tire burning furiously, roll past him, strike a ridge and bound high, flaring against the night sky. He rose and ran on, dimly aware of fire sparkling around him. He fell, and rose, and ran again. . . .

He lay with his face against rock, hearing a dull angry roaring that grew, drowned the rush of the fire. Light glared suddenly in his face, blinding him, rushing at him from the darkness ahead.

A high, dark silhouette loomed beside him, halted with a clatter of metal, an angry backfiring of immense idling engines. It was a tank, the dusty white star on its side gleaming dully in the flickering light. David saw the blue beam of the aliens come to bear on it, saw smoke boil up as the metal grew cherry red—

The turret moved, clanking, with a whine of servo motors, the long snout of the 20mm cannon depressed, came to bear on the fantastic vessel confronting it. There was a flash, an ear-bursting bellow. The tank skidded backward two feet, driven by the recoil—and two hundred feet distant, the alien vessel rocked as the high explosive shell detonated against it. And as the smoke cleared, David saw a ragged rent in the smooth curve of the craft's side. Again the tank's gun spoke, and from beyond it, another gun roared, and still another. The blue beam jerked away from its first target, seeking easier prey. David saw it glare on a second tank, hold on the vehicle's gun muzzle—

With a blast that shook the ground, the target tank exploded, filling the air with screaming shrapnel; the heat ray had touched off the shell in the chamber. But the firing from the other tank went on, faster now, as more machines came up, each adding its voice to the battle. And abruptly, with a hissing crackle audible even above the thunder of the guns, the invading ship caught fire, in an instant was an incandescent tower of corruscating fury, boiling up into the Hallowe'en sky. . . .

Silence fell. Men were clambering down from the tanks, their faces ruddy in the glare of that fierce blaze. David tried to stand, to call, but only a hoarse croak sounded. He felt himself falling, and once again, darkness closed in. . .

5

*A dream* David thought. *I'm dead, and dreaming.* . . . And then there were hands on him, faces that bent over him, voices that spoke words he understood:

". . . this guy here! Looks like he's hurt bad!"

". . . what outfit?"

"Must be from the Air Guard unit. Get him out of there. . ."

". . . easy. Lay him up there, fellows. . ."

Then there was a jarring, bumping ride; vague, ghostly bumps, that David hardly felt. He lay on his back, looking up at a curve of brown cloth above him. He turned his head, saw a man in torn and dusty olive drab, his arm bandaged, a splint on his leg. Another wounded man lay on his other side. He was in an Army ambulance—or a truck, converted to temporary use. . . .

Voices sounded near him:

". . .don't get it, Lieutenant. We come barrelling out here on account of we get word some wiseacre's headed this way in a stolen 'track. About the time we think we've got him—shooting stars, yet, the whole sky full of 'em! And then—that—whatever it was! I seen it with my own eyes, and I still couldn't tell you whether I was seeing things or—well, you tell me, Lieutenant, what did we see out there?"

"I didn't see a thing, Sarge." a hard-bitten voice came back. "And if you're smart, neither did you."

"Huh? But we fired on it—the whole outfit—"

"We fired on the spot where the tracers were going in. We got the command to open up, and we did. That's all I know."

"Yeah, but—"

"The major's in command. Maybe he saw something—he could never prove it now. Let him write the report. You and me, Sarge—we're just a couple of dumb armor-jockeys, right?"

"Yeah—I see what you mean. . . ."

"How're they doing in back?"

There was a pause. David sensed a flashlight beam flicking over him. He lay still and silent.

"No change. Funny about the fly boy. I wonder how he got mixed in this?"

"Let the Air Force explain that one."

"Yeah. Yeah, that's right. Me, I don't know nothing. . . ."

David raised himself on one elbow. In the

darkness, a wounded man groaned softly. He crawled carefully over the man, fighting back the dizziness, looked out through the open flap at the rear of the speeding truck. Dark empty hills flowed past. In the distance there were the lights of a small town. . . .

The truck slowed, turned right, lumbered up over a grade crossing. As it halted momentarily at the top, David slid over the tailgate, dropped into the ditch. He watched as the taillights of the truck dwindled away along the road. Then he rose and slowly, painfully, started for the distant lights.

He would find shelter there, lie up until his wounds and burns healed. He had money enough to quiet curiosity. He thought of Sergeant Anoti—dead, his body still lying where he had fallen, perhaps. One more casualty in the secret, silent war. A war not yet over, a war that for David Vincent would never end, until the last of the Invaders had been hunted down and killed.

Overhead, the stars looked down, indifferent.